THE BODY VANISHES

The Eleventh Little Indian

THE BODY VANISHES

Jacquemard-Sénécal

TRANSLATED BY GORDON LATTA

DODD, MEAD & COMPANY

NEW YORK

1   2   3   4   5   6   7   8   9   10

First published in France under the title
Le Crime de la Maison Grün

Library of Congress Cataloging in Publication Data

Jacquemard, Yves.
The body vanishes.

Translation of Le crime de la maison Grün.
I. Sénécal, Jean Michel, joint author. II. Title.
PZ4.J1764Bo 1980   [PQ2670.A249]   843'.914   80-17077
ISBN 0-396-07884-2

To Nathalie,
tenderly

THE BODY VANISHES

FRIDAY

1

A shrill cry rent the autumn night. But Strasbourg, peace-
fully asleep, did not stir. It required a second piercing
scream from Madame Dickbauch for lights to begin
appearing in a number of windows in the Petite France
district of the town.

Presently, she was surrounded by a small crowd. By
this time she was near to fainting, and could only point a
trembling finger towards the bank of the river Ill, silvery
in the moonlight. At first sight there appeared to be
nothing there but a bundle of white rags, and a derisory
murmur was beginning to spread through the crowd but
just then a closer look established that the bundle was a
human body and, unfortunately, a dead one. Once this
fact was passed on to Madame Dickbauch she elected to
give a third scream, which resulted in more lights being
switched on and the arrival, in nightshirt and dressing-
gown, of Monsieur Gräber, the proprietor of a neigh-
bouring bar. His arrival was timely: Madame Dickbauch's frayed nerves required the immediate consump-
tion of some kind of alcoholic restorative, which he was
able and willing to supply on the spot.

On further inspection the corpse proved to be that of a
young woman, with long red hair that floated on the surface of the water and wavered gently to the rhythm of the

current. The tall reeds growing by the river's edge had wrapped themselves round the body as though in a last embrace, saving it from going under or drifting downstream. Inevitably, there was someone to suggest removing it to a drier place and someone else to counter this by saying that everything should be left exactly as it was until the police arrived. Finally the small group decided to adopt the second proposal. The cold had begun to penetrate their inadequate clothing, and a move was made to Gräber's bar to restore their circulation with bottles of kirsch and, as a secondary consideration, to telephone the police.

When the police arrived they were confronted by the memorable spectacle of the worthy Madame Dickbauch seated on a table, holding forth in the midst of an indescribable hubbub, while the atmosphere grew dense with pipe-smoke, and a smiling Monsieur Gräber opened a fourth bottle of kirsch.

The appearance of Superintendent Dullac, accompanied by his subordinates, produced an immediate and respectful silence. Despite her sixty-seven years, Madame Dickbauch jumped off the table with surprising suppleness and sat down modestly in a chair, as was more fitting for her age.

Still no more than thirty-five, Dullac was young for a Superintendent. He had been born in Paris, where he had received a sound education and had shown a natural aptitude for mathematics, philosophy and various subsidiary subjects requiring the exercise of logic. Paradoxically, he was given to making remarks wholly lacking in logic, gems of absurdity that amused his friends and led them to suspect that he was 'not quite right in the head'. But in this they completely misjudged him. The truth was that these flights into surrealism only occurred when he was in a state of abstraction and wholly taken up with his professional problems. His normal expression was that of a cheerful, perpetually smiling clown, though the beginnings of a paunch and already pronounced baldness were slowly transforming it into that of a fond, indulgent parent.

This prepossessing appearance and the occasional vagaries in his speech combined to make him extremely likeable, which proved a considerable advantage to him in his investigations and had proved even more helpful in getting himself accepted by the citizens of Strasbourg when he had been transferred to the large Alsatian town some five years earlier. To the mistrust that even the most law-abiding citizens evince towards police officers had been added the mistrust of the Alsatian population for a Parisian who had been thrust on them out of the blue. They had begun by playing tricks on him, making a point of addressing him in the Alsatian dialect, which he had had no opportunity to learn, though it was in common usage in the town. His subordinates, nearly all of them born locally, had translated for him while laughing up their sleeves; naturally on the side of their fellow-citizens, they were no doubt also jealous of a promotion that they considered should have come to one of themselves. But little by little his innate courtesy, his good humour, and the tact and competence which he had brought to bear in solving two or three difficult cases had overcome the antagonism. And when he entered Gräber's bar on the night in question, just before dawn, he saw scarcely anyone who was not a friend among the rubicund faces, glowing as much from kirsch as emotion, as they turned towards him with obvious relief.

'Poor Madame Dickbauch!' he said sympathetically. 'From what I hear, you must have had a nasty shock.'

Madame Dickbauch was a well-known character in the Petite France district. A retired post office employee, she looked after the welfare of an army of stray cats which, but for her kindness, would have long ago ended up in the river like the unfortunate young woman she had just come across. As she was far from well off – post office pensions having little in common with golden handshakes – there was no possibility of her feeding fifty cats or more from her own resources; consequently, she was reduced to getting up very early each morning before the dustmen began their rounds, and making a tour of the dustbins, from which she extracted sufficient nourishment to satisfy her hungry protégés. This did not cause her any undue inconvenience, as she suffered from insomnia and was of a romantic disposition, two essential requirements for dedicated night-prowlers.

Since she knew Dullac to be aware of the purpose of her nocturnal expeditions she did not need to waste any time in explaining what a woman of her unimpeachable respectability had been doing wandering round the picturesque byways of Petite France at four o'clock in the morning, and could embark immediately on her sensational narrative. In a quavering voice designed to conceal her pleasure at playing such a leading part in the drama, she recounted how, her charitable mission accomplished, she had been returning home by the esplanade that ran along the river bank when, level with the end of the Dentelles cul-de-sac, where the esplanade had become a footbridge, she had suddenly spotted . . . the corpse.

At this juncture Dullac, a methodical man, decided to view the body and the site where it lay before hearing anything further. He set out, followed by the small group from the bar, and reached the spot in a matter of minutes. And it was then that the witnesses recognized and regretted their inexperience: if they had not dragged the body out of the water, they should at least have left someone behind to keep an eye on it. But their regrets had come too late, and were completely useless; as though tired of waiting, the dead woman had disappeared.

2

'Well, now!' Dullac observed mildly. 'It looks as if you've all been dreaming.'

He would have been glad if they had. A death by drowning was never a pleasant occurrence with which to be faced. All the same, it was scarcely credible for some twenty people to have suffered from a hallucination at one and the same time. So his observation had merely been rhetorical, designed to get the inquiry going again, which it did by eliciting firm assurances from his audience that the corpse had not been a figment of their imaginations.

Dawn was beginning to break over Strasbourg and, with the cold becoming increasingly bitter, they had all been forced to return to the bar. After apologizing to

everyone for detaining them, and by now almost as
exhausted as they were, Dullac was trying to take stock of
the situation.

A second hypothesis, more rational than the first,
occurred to him: the current had finally disentangled the
body and carried it down towards the Pont Saint-Martin,
perhaps even further. The obvious step to take was to send
police out to search the river, and he immediately gave the
appropriate orders.

Turning back to his audience, he sighed, 'If only you'd
moved the body further up the bank!'

Wetzel, the owner of a local picture-gallery, pointed
out, 'We were afraid to. In detective stories, they always
say one should leave things exactly as they are.'

'And it wouldn't have been very convenient,' Gräber
put in. 'We were on the bridge and the body was floating
by the foot of the Dentelles cul-de-sac. It would have
meant going a long way round.'

Dullac nodded. The footbridge to which Gräber
referred, constructed on piles, started in the Place
Benjamin-Zix, a short way from the bar, strayed out into
the middle of the Ill, turned partly back again to run
parallel with the houses overlooking the river, and finally
returned to the bank, where it became transformed into a
shady esplanade. Consequently, pedestrians walking
along the bridge were separated by several yards from the
buildings, the walls of which descended to the river's edge,
as well as from the small Dentelles cul-de-sac that jutted
out perpendicularly from the road of the same name. And
it was close by the end of this lane that Madame Dickbauch had spotted the body.

There was still one final question for Dullac to ask, perhaps the most important one of all.

'Now, my good friends, please listen carefully. If there's anyone here who thinks he recognized the dead woman or even has a vague idea of who she may be, I want him to say so at once. I shan't regard it as a formal statement; merely as a lead that may save me a lot of time and trouble.'

His audience looked at each other but remained silent. Then, hesitatingly, glancing around as though to solicit approval from the others, Wetzel spoke up. 'Well, you know . . . It seemed to me . . . Mind you, I may be completely wrong . . . '

'Yes, that's quite understood,' Dullac assured him. 'As I just said, you're not on oath. All you're doing is giving me a friendly tip.'

'In that case, Superintendent, I'll tell you what I've been thinking for the last hour. There aren't many women around here with long red hair and it struck me that I'd seen the tight-fitting white blouse and long black skirt before.'

'Me, too,' Gräber murmured.

'And me,' Madame Dickbauch asserted, not wanting to be thrust into the background.

Several of the others nodded and a name began to be circulated in a low whisper. Finally, Wetzel announced audibly, 'Dyana Pasquier.'

Surprised, Dullac repeated, 'Dyana Pasquier? You mean . . . '

'Yes, Superintendent; Denis Grün's fiancée.'

3

All these proceedings had taken up a certain time and it was close on six o'clock in the morning when Dullac rang the Grüns' front-door bell. The old Alsatian mansion, now completely renovated and modernized, had housed several generations of the Grün family of fine-art book-binders, a family one hundred per cent *Strasbourgeois*, of which the present head bore the striking name of Wotan. It occupied an enviable site alongside the river, standing at an angle to the Rue des Dentelles and facing the Place Benjamin-Zix.

The ground floor was wholly taken up by a spacious shop and an equally spacious workroom leading out of it. In the shop Wotan displayed and sold rare books, some of them in the original bindings which he had restored, others in bindings that were entirely his own work. In both cases they were *objets d'art* of great beauty, thanks to his outstanding talent, and greatly appreciated by Stras-bourg connoisseurs. The benefits from this were two-fold: he was able to maintain his large house, and he was respected by the artistic members of the community, whom he had organized into a discussion group that met every Thursday evening in his shop and workroom and over which he presided.

The entrance to the shop was in the Rue des Dentelles; the workroom windows looked out on to the river; and the front door to the private section of the house was in the square. A door in the hall gave access to the shop, while a staircase led up to the other two floors.

The first floor was taken up by the large, comfortable flat that Wotan occupied with his young wife, Edwige. On the second floor there was a smaller flat and a studio flat: the flat belonged to Wotan's son, Denis, who lived there with his girl-friend, Dyana Pasquier; the studio flat was leased to a pleasant retired police officer with the charming name of Noel Loiseau. Above them was an enormous loft to which there was no visible access – the old worm-eaten staircase having been long since removed – but a handle on the second-floor landing opened a trap-door and released a retractable ladder, up which Denis and his elder sister, Claire, had climbed as children to enter an enchanted world, transformed by their imaginations into the setting for innumerable adventures.

Now twenty-three, Claire lived in Paris but paid frequent visits to her father and stepmother, the latter only a year or so older than herself, with whom she got on reasonably well. She had been staying in Strasbourg on one of these visits for the past fortnight, occupying the room in her father's flat that had been hers as a young girl.

Dullac pressed the bell. He could hear it ring but it did not appear to produce any reaction from inside the house and he had to ring again, wait, and ring a third time before the door opened to reveal the impressive figure of Wotan Grün himself.

When his parents – now a long time deceased – had christened their son Wotan they certainly could not have foreseen, both being of slender build, that their offspring as he grew up would inherit the gigantic stature of his great-grandfather Grün, whose memory the family cherished in the depths of their hearts, and his portrait in the depths of their loft. But chance, for once, had arranged things admirably; the Christian name of Wotan, which would have been ridiculous on a puny or ordinary-looking man, was wholly appropriate to this giant; huge, strong, and immensely virile despite his stoutness, with his thick black hair, short beard, bull-neck and wrestler's shoulders.

At the sight of him his great success with women was no longer surprising; nor was his recent second marriage, at the age of fifty, to a young woman from Colmar twenty-five years his junior.

'Well, now!' he exclaimed on discovering the Superintendent on his doorstep. 'If it isn't my friend Dullac!'

The sound of his voice, which matched the rest of his appearance, made the early-morning air quiver, and the Superintendent would not have been prepared to swear that the Cathedral bells had not reverberated at the same time.

With a welcoming gesture the giant beckoned him in: the two men had often met in the course of the last five years, and got on well together. They crossed the small hall with its imitation marble floor, on the right of which the broad staircase, also in imitation marble, rose to the upper storeys, and entered the shop.

By now daylight was stealing through the shutters, revealing the exquisitely bound books on display, together with a number of miniatures, old paintings and curios in which Grün dealt as a sideline. Being a Friday, Wotan had entertained his discussion group on the previous evening, but, thanks to Claire and Edwige, no traces remained; chairs, glasses, bottles and snacks had all been spirited away.

Perched on the edge of a chair that, according to Grün, had once been honoured by supporting Louis XIV's rump, Dullac wondered how he could tactfully introduce the matter that had brought him there. Fortunately, Wotan, unable to curb his surprise at this early visit, came to his assistance.

'Something wrong?' he inquired genially, though there was a faint undertone of anxiety in his voice.

'There may be . . . And it would help me if you'd answer my questions before asking yours.'

'All right, go ahead.'

'Have you seen Dyana recently?'

'Why? Has something happened to her?' Wotan's expression had not changed, but Dullac knew his man: though he would be too proud to reveal his fears, he must already be secretly dreading bad news.

'Wotan . . . please answer my question.'

'Depends on what you mean by recently. I saw her yesterday evening about six. I didn't see her after that: she didn't come to our meeting or to the Weberstub.'

'You spent the rest of the evening at the Weberstub?' Dullac knew it to be Wotan's favourite restaurant.

'As usual.'

'Was Denis with you?'

'Of course not!' The corners of Wotan's mouth twisted up in a wry grimace.

'Silly question,' Dullac admitted.

Nearly all Strasbourg was aware that Denis and his father were not on the best of terms, and in the natural

course of events it had come to Dullac's ears. Apart from
his fair hair, the young man took after Wotan physically;
his height and muscular build fully justified his father's
frequent boast: 'You can see he's a Grün, can't you?' But
in character he resembled his dead mother, a shy and diffi-
dent woman, and was continually crossing swords with
his father on matters of ideology.

Now that he was twenty-one and in his third year at the
university, he leaned towards the left in his political sym-
pathies, a fact which, depending on his mood of the
moment, caused his father to lose his temper or give a
despairing shrug. But Denis's main preoccupation was to
achieve a degree in modern history, and he scorned the
social life in which Wotan took such pleasure; most of his
time was spent at home studying or with his friend and
fellow-student, Charles Feldmann, who had a room in the
centre of the town, where they could indulge in endless
arguments without fear of interruption.

'I've no idea how Denis spent the evening,' Wotan said
sourly. 'The best way to find out would be to ask him.'

'Then I'll go up and see him, if I may?'

'At this hour? Is it as important as all that?'

Wotan was a strong enough man to stand shocks:
Dullac saw no point in stalling further. 'It's by no means
certain . . . Just supposition at the moment . . . '

'Come out with it, man!' Wotan snapped.

'Well, I've reason to fear that Dyana may have had a
fatal accident.'

Wotan remained silent for a moment. Though he must
have been struggling to master his profound anxiety,
Dullac saw nothing on his granite face to betray it

Finally, Wotan said, 'Very well, we'll go up.'

They returned to the hall and rapidly climbed the stone staircase. On the second floor Wotan rang the door-bell on his right. They did not have long to wait before Denis jerked the door open. His face was haggard and he was fully dressed; it was apparent that he had not slept all night. Before either of the two men could speak, he said distractedly to his father, 'Dyana hasn't come back.'

Then he seemed to become aware of the detective's presence and broke off, in too much of a daze to stand aside and let his visitors come in. It took a sharp word from his father to snap him out of it and induce him to lead the way into the living-room, where he collapsed on to the sofa, which still bore the imprint of his body. No doubt he had spent the night there, awake and waiting, as was evidenced by an ashtray filled with stubs, and a book by Hegel lying open on the floor.

'You mean you haven't seen her all night?' his father asked.

'She . . . she hasn't come back,' Denis repeated, as if he had not taken in the question.

Wotan began to show signs of exasperation. 'Get a grip of yourself, for God's sake! Try and act like an adult for once! What happened? Did you have a row?'

'What makes you think we did?'

'It's been known to happen. Can't you give me a straight answer?'

'Well, yes . . . She rushed out . . . '

'What time was it?'

'I can't remember exactly. Just before eleven, I think. At first I imagined that she'd gone to join you at the

Weberstub. But she hasn't come back,' he repeated for the third time, as though unable to detach his mind from this obsession.

'So that's why you asked if she were with us when we got back last night?'

'What time was that?' Dullac inquired. They were the first words he had spoken, being content up till then to watch and listen.

'The same as usual; just after half-past two,' Wotan answered. 'Edwige was tired. My daughter walked back with us. Then, as I was about to open the door of my flat on the first floor, Denis leaned over the banisters and asked if Dyana was with us.'

'Didn't it surprise you at that time of night?'

'Not in the least! As you know, Dyana's an usherette at the Lorelei cinema, and Thursday's her day off. But she seldom takes advantage of it to have an early night. She often goes round to friends of hers where they mess about cooking, drinking, smoking and gossiping, and stays till very late. All the same, she's never come back later than three.'

'She left in a temper,' Denis mumbled resentfully.

'It's your own fault. You ought to have married her a long time ago: I've told you often enough. Once you're married, small disagreements don't work up into quarrels.'

'I'm too young to get married.'

Wotan raised his arms in a gesture of despair and appealed to Dullac. 'What can one do? He's been going on like that for the last four years, ever since he met the girl. He loves her, he's living with her, but he refuses to marry her.' He turned on his son, savagely mimicking his tone of voice. ' "I'm too young! I'm too young!" You're a fool! What's more, someone who feels as strongly about morality as you do should begin by setting an example himself. Otherwise he's scarcely in a position to criticize his father's behaviour.' Wotan turned back to Dullac. 'I've stopped paying any attention to his snide remarks about Edwige's age. And at least I married her!'

'And are unfaithful to her every chance you get,' Denis muttered.

'Once again, what right have you to criticize? Edwige is perfectly happy. She's never run away from me or felt the need to sleep with anyone else. That's more than can be said for Dyana. Where is she now, for instance?'

'At Martine's, I expect,' Denis answered.

Surprised, his two visitors glanced at each other. Then, after a moment's reflection, Wotan said more calmly, 'Well, yes, that's possible,' and went on to explain to Dullac, 'Martine is Dyana's closest friend: she's an usherette at the Lorelei, too. If Dyana left here at eleven she'd have been in time to pick Martine up at the cinema after the last showing and go back with her.' He added sharply to his son, 'Go round to Martine and see.'

'I won't give Martine that pleasure,' Denis retorted. 'She'll be delighted I had a row with Dyana: she loathes me.'

'You ought to see your wife doesn't make friends with people like that.'

'She isn't my wife,' Denis pointed out sulkily.

Wotan appealed to Dullac again. 'Can you wonder I get exasperated? If you'll wait a minute, I'll come with you to

Martine's and I bet we'll find Dyana there.'

'It seems quite probable,' Dullac admitted. 'I certainly hope so.'

Leaving Denis free to return to his cherished Hegel they went down to the first floor. Outside the front door of his flat, Wotan put a finger to his lips. 'Edwige and Claire will still be asleep. Do you mind waiting out here while I get dressed? . . . Or I've a better idea. I dare say you could do with a cup of coffee?'

'I won't say no.'

'Then let's slip into the kitchen and have some together there.'

The kitchen windows looked on the river and the view was magnificent. Wotan filled a kettle with water and put it on to boil, then went out to get dressed, while Dullac sat down by a window and gazed out at the panorama. Below him was the river and to his right lay the Place Benjamin-Zix with its shady trees and famous headquarters of the Tanners' Guild, which in an hour or two would be receiving its usual influx of tourists: to his left was the foot-bridge, and beyond it the Pont Saint-Martin and the Weberstub. Though frosty, the weather promised to be fine and bracing.

Was it possible, he wondered, that the woman drowned in the river was not Dyana Pasquier after all? If so, who was she? As Wetzel had said, there was no profusion of redheads in the district, so perhaps she was a stranger from elsewhere? But if she were Dyana, how had it happened? Hurrying to join the others at the Weberstub, had she slipped in the darkness, fallen into the river and drowned? Or had she plunged into the river in a sudden fit of despair? Admittedly she had had a tiff with Denis, but you don't kill yourself because of a tiff. It was clear, despite his listless manner, that the young man loved Dyana and was hurt by her running out on him. And if he, Dullac, could sense the boy's affection for her, she must surely have been aware of it, too, whatever arguments they might have had.

His reflections were disrupted as he gradually became conscious that Wotan had returned, dressed to go out, and was extolling at some length the taste, bouquet and quality of freshly-made coffee.

'Yes, yes,' he said a shade impatiently, 'fresh coffee isn't warmed-up coffee.'

Wotan's burst of Homeric laughter finally brought him back to his present surroundings. 'What's the matter? What did I say?'

'You made a profound observation, my friend. As happens from time to time.'

When Wotan repeated his remark, Dullac good-naturedly joined in his laughter, though with rather less gusto. Then the two of them sat down at the oak table, facing each other, to enjoy the fragrant coffee, with fresh cream and slices of buttered bread. They were just finishing when the door opened to admit a young woman in jeans and a pullover, good-looking in rather a boyish way, whose energetic, explicit gestures recalled Wotan's. Dullac had met Claire Grün before and was used to her somewhat acid turn of speech, so he was not taken aback to hear her comment casually, 'Surprise, surprise! Cops on toast for breakfast?'

When this sally, not remarkable for its taste or wit,

merely produced a shrug from her father and an amiable 'Good morning, mademoiselle' from Dullac, she headed for the stove and set about warming up the coffee.

'Having a rest?' Dullac inquired.

'An involuntary one. I haven't any work at the moment.'

Claire produced and directed shows for the smaller night-clubs in Paris. They were sophisticated, topical and witty, generally consisting of skits, songs and dances from three or four promising young performers. She possessed genuine talent, inherited from her father, and enjoyed considerable success. Unlike her brother, she was a true Grün.

As she brought her steaming cup over to the table and sat down, she observed, 'I promised Dyana I'd go shopping with her this morning.'

Dullac glanced at Wotan. He would have preferred not to alarm the young woman while they were not yet in possession of the facts, but Wotan chose to speak out.

'Dyana didn't sleep here last night. We don't know where she is.'

Claire received the news calmly. 'She's probably with Martine. I suppose she had another row with Denis?'

'I'm afraid so.'

'She's got the patience of a saint. That fool Denis doesn't realize how lucky he is.'

'He's certainly got no sense of humour,' Wotan grumbled.

'What can you expect? He's a Marxist!'

'And you aren't?' Dullac asked blandly.

Claire's eyebrows rose. 'Anything but . . . There was a

time when people were keen on Marx, but now he's completely passé. It isn't the economic struggle that matters today but the need to reassess all the traditional moral values.'

'With Women's Lib in the forefront of the battle?' Dullac suggested with faint irony.

Faint or not, it was perceptible to Claire, who was no fool, and her only answer consisted of a supercilious glance.

'How lucky I am in my children!' Wotan broke in. 'One's a red and the other's an anarchist!'

'It's only a phase,' Dullac said consolingly.

'Oh, sure!' Claire snapped. 'We'll grow out of it when we're older, the same as we grew out of acne!'

'Enough of that, now!' Wotan said, afraid that the Superintendent might finally get annoyed. 'It's time we were off.' He got up, and Dullac followed suit.

'Where are you going?' Claire asked.

'We've some business to attend to.'

'State secret, is it?'

'If you like . . . By the way, if Dyana comes back, tell her to wait for me. I want to talk to her.'

'I've told you, she must be at Martine's.'

Wotan did not reply. Dullac said goodbye to the young woman, who condescended to smile at him – a very attractive smile, he noticed – and the two men left the flat.

They had scarcely started downstairs before Wotan turned to his companion. 'Now I want the truth. What exactly are you afraid has happened to Dyana? And what made you come here?'

Dullac saw that he could no longer be evasive; anyway,

there was no proof that the woman found in the river actually was Dyana Pasquier. So he proceeded to tell Wotan the events of the night before.

Some of the colour drained from Wotan's face. 'I hope to God those people were mistaken! It would be terrible for Denis,' he muttered. 'But if Wetzel was one of them . . . Wetzel's a friend of ours and a member of my discussion group: he knows Dyana very well. It's hard to imagine he could be wrong.'

'It was in the middle of the night, don't forget: a clear night, admittedly, but still night. And she was lying face downwards. It's too soon to give up hope.'

'How was she dressed?'

'According to those who saw her, in a tight-fitting white blouse and a long black skirt,' Dullac answered; then, as Wotan let a faint exclamation escape him, asked, 'What's wrong?'

'That's exactly how Dyana often dresses.'

'So do hundreds of other girls in Strasbourg. Come along to Martine's place with me. You'll find Dyana there safe and sound and you'll have been worrying for nothing.'

Wotan nodded and continued on his way downstairs. When they reached the hall, he halted. 'I must get some money from the safe. Will you wait a moment?'

Taking the Superintendent's assent for granted, he went into the shop, where the two men had been an hour earlier, crossed over to the right and opened the large door to the workroom, which was secured by a stout, old-fashioned lock. A few seconds later, Dullac heard him give a hoarse cry, then call out to him, 'Quick! Come here!'

He hurried into the workroom, wondering what disaster could have occurred; Wotan was not easily roused to such a pitch of excitement.

Daylight was filtering through the closed shutters sufficiently for him to take in every detail. The huge room was in complete disorder. The safe had been spared but the cupboards, racks and drawers were all wide open and empty, their contents strewn about the floor. But this was not the worst.

A body lay stretched out at full length in the middle of the confusion, a lifeless body that Dullac recognized immediately.

Dyana Pasquier.

4

'It doesn't make sense!' Inspector Holz protested to his superior officer. 'A body that turns up, disappears and then turns up again! I hope it's not going to disappear again, too!'

'Hardly likely this time,' Dullac said placidly.

They were in his office at Police Headquarters, passing the time in none-too-fruitful conjectures as they waited for the autopsy report.

'Then we're faced with the stock question,' Holz observed. 'Murder, suicide or accident?'

'If the body hadn't disappeared and reappeared in that extraordinary way, murder would have seemed to be ruled out,' Dullac commented.

'Whereas now it's almost a certainty.'

'I wouldn't go as far as that. Someone certainly decided to drag the body out of the river and then dump it in Grün's workroom. But we don't know that that someone was a murderer.'

'If he hadn't killed her, why move the body?'

'You could ask the same question if he *had* killed her, and with better reason. When it was highly probable that the death would be attributed to accident or suicide, why not leave well alone?'

'Very well, then, I'll go back to my original question. If it *wasn't* murder, why move the body?'

'Perhaps to distract attention from the other aspect of the affair, the more important one.'

'Meaning?'

'*The burglary.*'

'The burglary! But what was stolen? Just a few old books . . . '

Dullac looked up at his assistant and sighed. 'I'm sorry to have to say it, Holz, but you're a philistine. Those old books, as you call them, were worth thousands of francs. There was a fifteenth-century *incunabulum*, an early printed book, among them that might fetch over a million francs.'

'If that's so, who could a burglar flog them to?'

'Now there you've got a point. He'd need to find an unscrupulous collector. Quite a quantity of gold leaf was stolen as well.'

'Ah!'

'Yes, that makes sense to you. You can understand people wanting to steal gold, but books are beyond you. You're a philistine, Holz.'

'You've just told me that,' Holz pointed out, somewhat ruffled.

Dullac grinned. 'Don't take it to heart. You've other sterling qualities or I wouldn't have picked you as my assistant. One curious thing is that the bulk of the gold leaf was locked up in the safe and it's still there: the safe wasn't forced. And it doesn't look as if anyone even tried to force it. Interesting, eh?'

'You mean it wasn't a professional job?'

'It obviously hadn't been carefully planned beforehand. Otherwise the safe would have been forced, or at least there would have been marks on it. And there wasn't any attempt to force the door into the shop: nothing was stolen from there. Seems pretty amateurish to me.'

'Why hadn't Grün locked up all the gold leaf and the more valuable books in the safe?'

'I asked him that. The safe is too small to hold all the valuable books and the *incunabulum* wouldn't go in, anyway. As regards the gold leaf, Grün was entertaining his discussion group, as he did every Thursday, and some of his friends asked him to let them see and handle the leaves he uses for gilding. Gold in that form is a rarity people don't often come across, so it naturally arouses their curiosity. Then, at half-past ten, when everyone left to go home or to the Weberstub, Grün didn't bother to put the gold leaves back in the safe.'

'Very careless of him.'

'I agree. So does he.'

'Was he the last person to leave the workroom and the shop?'

'No. Edwige, his wife, and his daughter, Claire, stayed behind to clear up.'

'Couldn't they have put the leaves back in the safe?'

'They didn't know the combination. But all the doors are very solid and there's never been a theft of any kind from the workroom for as long as Grün remembers, so no one thought there was any risk, if they thought about it at all.'

'Talking of doors, how did the burglars get in?'

'They didn't break in: that's what's so puzzling. It looks as if they got in from the esplanade alongside the river.'

'You mean through the windows?'

'It's the only explanation. Those windows aren't barred and the shutters are pretty old. I imagine Claire and Edwige left the windows half-open when the meeting broke up to air the room. The shutters would have been closed, but I expect it would have been easy enough to open them from the outside. All one has to do is slip a knife-blade between the two panels and jerk the crossbar up.'

'How about shutting them again?'

'Same process in reverse. You support the crossbar on the knife-blade, pull the panels together again, withdraw the blade and the bar falls back into place.'

'And they brought the body in through the window, too?'

'Must have . . . You remember the witnesses said the body was lying in the water near the Grüns' house by the cul-de-sac? Well, maybe it was pure coincidence and an extraordinary piece of luck for the burglars. As they approached their objective they caught sight of the body, and the idea then occurred to them to remove it from the water and leave it in the workroom. That way the burglary would be linked with the corpse and our suspicions diverted from the one to the other.'

Holz frowned. 'Seems to me rather far-fetched.'

'I agree, if the only object of the burglary was to make some easy money. But not if it wasn't.'

'What other motive could they have had?'

'*Vengeance!*'

'Vengeance!' Holz repeated, startled.

'Yes. They may have had it in for the Grün family for some reason. In that case, the money would have just been a bonus.'

'But if your theory's right,' Holz objected, 'it would mean that the burglary took place after Madame Dickbauch discovered the body at half-past four.'

'That's right.'

'And before you turned up to find the body had disappeared.'

'That's to say, about five.'

'Do you really think that, in the space of half an hour, the burglars had time to arrive, open the shutters, pillage the workroom, carry the body up from the river, deposit it in the house and make off with the loot? What's more, the neighbourhood was crawling with people after the old woman started screaming.'

'The burglars wouldn't have known anything about that. When they got to work we were all in Gräber's bar. The streets were deserted and quiet again then.'

Holz thought for a moment, then exploded, 'No,

Superintendent, I really can't swallow it. It's too improbable.'

'Just as you like . . . Still, let's bear it in mind.'

'There is another possibility . . .'

'Go ahead!'

The Inspector chose his words carefully. 'I imagine all those books and things were well insured?'

'I know what you're leading up to. It had already occurred to me.'

'Well?'

'Grün has no need of the insurance money. His business is doing better than ever. He's simply rolling.'

'Who says so? Him?'

'No, me. He may be a friend of mine, but that doesn't mean I show him any favours. I checked up on his bank account. Besides, Wotan Grün's an intelligent man.'

'How does that come in?'

'*If he had burgled himself there would certainly have been signs of a break-in.*'

Holz gave a low whistle. 'Yes, I see . . .'

'Which leaves us just where we were,' Dullac pointed out wryly.

SATURDAY

1

The autopsy report was lying on Dullac's desk when he reached his office in the morning. And it was in the nature of a thunderbolt. He rang for Holz and announced curtly, 'Murder.'

'Good Lord!' Holz looked stunned, then pulled himself together and asked, 'How? Was she strangled? Poisoned? Or what?'

'Drowned. But it was murder just the same. There were still finger-marks on her neck, showing that her head had been held under water. They weren't clear enough for us to have spotted them, but they were there all right.'

'Filthy swine!' Holz muttered. 'She was such a lovely girl. Couldn't have been more than twenty-five.'

'It wouldn't have made things any better if it had been an old man,' Dullac pointed out.

From Holz's expression he did not appear to agree. He asked, 'Were they able to fix a time?'

'They're cautious, as usual. They say that death occurred between midnight and two in the morning: probably between half-past twelve and half-past one.'

'Denis Grün!' Holz exploded. 'It must have been him. He's one of those pretentious intellectual bastards. I could never stand the sight of him. And everyone knows he led that poor girl the hell of a life.'

'If you allow your personal feelings to run away with you you're going to be more of a hindrance than a help,' Dullac told him sharply.

'Sorry, Chief. Won't happen again.'

'In that case, you'd better come along with me. I'm going to call on the Grüns.'

2

As they approached the house through the square, a young man suddenly emerged from it and headed towards the esplanade. Dullac hailed him just before he turned the corner: 'Monsieur Schiller!'

Surprised, the young man turned round to face them. He was extremely good-looking, with greyish-blue eyes, fair hair and a disarming smile.

'I'm Superintendent Dullac and this is Inspector Holz. Could we have a few words with you?'

'Is it about Dyana?' He spoke with a strong and attractive Alsatian accent.

'Yes. Can you come back to the house for a minute or two?'

'If you like. I've nothing particular to do.'

'Good!' Followed by the other two, Dullac skirted the house and went into the shop. They greeted the salesgirl as they passed through and went upstairs to the first floor.

It was Edwige who opened the door of the flat to them. A tall young woman, only just twenty-five, she already displayed a mature, almost haughty type of Germanic beauty, with her limpid eyes, long flaxen hair falling down her back and the milky sheen of her skin. Earning Dullac's unspoken approval, she had not plunged into deep mourning but, rejecting black as she always rejected any conspicuous colour, was wearing a simple grey woollen dress. But no one could fail to notice the grief and shock clouding her usual serene expression.

'Jacques!' she exclaimed in surprise as she caught sight of Schiller.

'I met these two gentlemen as I went out,' he explained. 'Is Claire still here?'

'Yes, you'll find her in her room, where you left her.'

'If I may, I'll call you if I need you,' Dullac said to him and the young man went down the corridor towards the back of the flat.

'You'll find my husband in his study,' Edwige told Dullac, then added, 'If you've got bad news, please break it to him gently. Wotan's a strong man, but we're all badly shaken by this tragedy.'

She spoke with an unaffectedness that gave the words additional force. Dullac, who had already met her on numerous occasions, was scarcely aware of it, but it did not escape Holz, who promptly decided that the second Madame Grün was a woman to be reckoned with.

The two men moved on to Wotan's study, where they found him seated at his desk, running through the morning's mail. He had apparently expected Dullac's visit, for he displayed no surprise, and merely exclaimed, 'Well?'

'Well . . . ' Dullac began, but Wotan immediately cut him short with a sharp gesture and demanded bluntly, 'Was it murder?'

Dullac nodded. 'I'm afraid so.'

Wotan got up slowly and walked over to the window, where he rested his forehead against the glass, contemplating the Rue des Dentelles and the houses opposite. Presently, jabbing one finger after another into the palm of his hand as though counting, he pronounced, 'Bereavement, every kind of complication, burglary and scandal . . . '

'I know. You have to be tough to face it,' Dullac said. Wotan swung round. 'Do I strike you as a weakling?'

Even in these circumstances, Dullac had difficulty in repressing a smile. There was certainly nothing in Wotan's indomitable façade to arouse compassion.

'Now, then,' he said, sitting down at his desk again and waving his visitors to chairs facing him. 'First things first. What proof have you got that she was murdered?'

He was obviously determined to take charge of the investigation himself, and Dullac was too intelligent to resent it. He knew Wotan sufficiently well to be aware that he took his position as head of the family very seriously, and that he would be regarding himself as responsible for each and every member of it. So he answered quite readily, 'Dyana was definitely drowned. But in keeping her head under in the Ill, the murderer left marks on her neck that showed up in the course of the autopsy. But for that, we should no doubt have been unable to prove that it wasn't a case of accident or suicide.'

'Showing that there's no such thing as a perfect crime,' Wotan commented. 'And now I suppose that all the members of my family are under suspicion?' He did not wait for an answer, but went on, 'Yes, that goes without saying

... Well, you can count on me to give you any help I can.'

'Thank you. I appreciate that,' Dullac said and meant it. He had always found the older man an engaging character, and the dignity and self-control he was now exhibiting increased his liking for him.

Wotan continued evenly, 'I imagine the first thing you'll want to know is how the members of my family spent the day of the murder. You'll see each of them in turn. Claire's in her bedroom and Edwige is in hers. No doubt, you've already told them not to leave the house?'

'I hardly liked to do that until I'd spoken to you,' Dullac answered with his habitual courtesy.

'Then I'll tell them for you,' Wotan said, getting up. 'Wait for me here. I'll only be a minute. If you feel like a drink, help yourselves.' He gestured towards a small bar in a corner of the room and made an exit worthy of a star from the Comédie-Française.

'What an amazing man he is!' Holz remarked. 'It's the first time I've come in contact with him. What with him and his wife we aren't going to have too easy a time of it.'

'The daughter, Claire, takes after him. We shouldn't have so much trouble with Denis. He's a bit of a weakling.'

'And Jacques Schiller? Where does he come in?'

'He's Claire's boy-friend. I thought you knew.'

'I did know,' Holz said quickly, resenting any reflection on his knowledge of local gossip. 'The Grün children don't seem too keen on marriage.'

At this moment Wotan returned. He shut the door carefully behind him, wishing, no doubt, to ensure that the conversation he was about to have with the two detectives was not overheard by the rest of the family. He sat down again behind his broad desk, and, with his elbows resting on the blotter and his fingers joined in an arch, announced, 'The ladies will wait till you want to see them. And so will that little whipper-snapper Schiller whom I found with my daughter. Charming boy, actually: no prospects, but very aesthetic.'

'I suppose it's that last quality that attracts Claire,' Dullac ventured.

'Of course!' Wotan roared in his stentorian voice. 'You'll have noticed how determined she is to remain free and independent. I can't see her ever saddling herself with a husband. However, that's their business. Let's get on with ours.'

At this second attempt by Wotan to take charge, Dullac decided that it was time to assert his own authority a little. Employing a more official tone of voice than he had up till now, he said, 'I shall want to see your son, too.'

Wotan was too shrewd not to catch on. 'And you shall, Superintendent,' he said with mock deference. 'Denis has remained in his room ever since he heard the distressing news. You'll go up to him later when you've finished your inquiries on this floor.'

For a few seconds, their eyes met and Dullac was the first to look away.

'And now for my movements on Thursday,' Wotan continued. 'As I think I told you already, the last time I saw Dyana alive was at six o'clock. Edwige and I were in the drawing-room watching television. Dyana rang, Claire let her in and she came and sat with us for a few minutes.'

'Did she look quite normal?'

'Absolutely. By that I mean she looked exhausted.'

'So she often got over-tired?'

'In my opinion, it's always best to have a conventional job; one where you work during the day and sleep at night. I admit I stay up late myself, but then I sleep late into the morning. What with the afternoon and evening shows, Dyana used to get very tired at the cinema. That being so, the sensible thing to have done would have been to sleep late, too. But she did nothing of the sort: she went for walks, shopped or dropped in on her friends. On top of that, of course, she did all her household chores. I suggested to her several times that she should change her job. With my contacts, I could have easily found her an interesting one: once I even suggested that she should serve in the shop, but she wanted to be independent and turned my offer down. It was then that I took on Florence.'

'How long had she known your son?'

'Four years. But the two of them have only been living here for the last three.'

'Where did they live before that?'

'In one of the rooms in town allocated to students.'

'But your second-floor flat was vacant, wasn't it?'

'Yes, but Dyana and Denis both felt the same. Their pride, they told me, wouldn't allow them to be beholden to me. Young idiots! To avoid being indebted to me, Denis lived for a year sponging on his girl-friend. She was already working at the Lorelei then and was the breadwinner.'

'Hasn't the position been just the same recently?'

'No, quite different; because Denis's scholastic successes at the university gained him a grant, and the grant, coupled with Dyana's salary, was enough for them to pay me a rent for the second-floor flat. I'd have willingly let them have it for nothing but they wouldn't hear of it.'

Dullac went back to where they had been before the diversion. 'So, when your daughter-in-law dropped in on you at six o'clock on Thursday evening, she gave you the impression of being tired. But apart from that?'

'Nothing else.'

'She didn't appear at all anxious?'

'Not anxious or annoyed or distressed. I tell you, she was her normal self.'

'And after sitting with you for a few minutes she left. What did you do then?'

'Claire was reading in her room. At about seven she went down to the workroom with Edwige to prepare it for our guests; put out the chairs, drinks and light refreshments, which we've been providing for the past ten years, ever since the discussion group came into existence. They came up again at eight o'clock and we had dinner.'

'Where were Dyana and Denis during this period?'

'In their own flat, I presume. We seldom dined together.'

'Forgive me for asking this question, but am I right in thinking that you and the young couple weren't on the best of terms?'

'No, it wasn't that.' Wotan gave the Superintendent a glance of mild reproof. 'The fact is, I admired Dyana's beauty and intelligence, and I was extremely proud of Denis's success at the university. But their way of life, their ideas, and their topics of conversation – everything about them – irritated and distressed me. You could say there was a certain incompatibility of outlook. But nothing more.'

Without making any comment, Dullac went on to ask, 'The discussion group met at eight-thirty, I believe?'

'Yes, that's correct. Our guests began to turn up at eight-thirty.'

'I'd like to have a list of them.' Dullac indicated Holz, who had produced a shorthand notebook and a pencil.

'Here's the list.' Wotan casually pushed a sheet of paper across his desk towards the detectives.

Annoyed at Wotan being a leap ahead of him, Dullac gave him a curt 'Thanks' and handed the sheet to Holz.

'An argument broke out almost at the start of the proceedings. I unfortunately said that propagandist art could never be true art. Most of the members agreed with me but some of the younger ones, led, I'm sorry to say, by my daughter, protested violently.'

'Well, if you don't share your children's ideas,' Dullac said with assumed ingenuousness, 'you at least have the satisfaction of knowing that they share each other's.'

'Don't you believe it!' Wotan roared, making the bibelots shake on their shelves. 'Claire never tires of calling her brother a narrow-minded, puritanical theorist, and he retorts by accusing her of being a deviationist, revisionist, and God knows what else. And when, with the laudable intention of calming things down, I venture to say that on the whole Claire's views seem easier to live with, he declares sarcastically that there may be hope for me yet. And at this point the two of them join forces to denounce me as an over-privileged, despicable, fossilized capitalist! I won't go into further details; you must have got the general picture.'

'All of which doesn't disguise the fact that you're extremely fond of them,' Dullac remarked.

'Of course I'm fond of them!' Wotan struck the polished top of his mahogany desk with his huge fists. 'They're Grüns, aren't they? How could I not be fond of them? But on this occasion Claire went too far. She turned what might have been an interesting discussion into a ridiculous scene. In the end, she stormed out of the room and only came back an hour later.'

'Calmed down?'

'Calmed down,' Wotan said drily with a mock gesture of relief that brought smiles to the detectives' faces. He went on, 'It must have been close on half-past ten. I know, because that's the time our meetings nearly always break up. Most of our friends went home, but two or three of them came on with me to end the evening at the Weberstub. Claire and Edwige stayed behind to put things away and leave the room tidy for the following morning. As you know, in the bustle of leaving I forgot to replace the gold leaf that I had taken out of the safe during the evening. Not that it has any importance. The burglary's a trivial matter in comparison with poor Dyana's death.'

'Did you go straight to the Weberstub?'

'Yes. We were there in under five minutes. Edwige joined us in a quarter of an hour, and Claire arrived shortly after.'

Surprised, Dullac asked, 'They didn't come together?'

'No. I don't know what kept Claire, but you've only to ask her.'

'How long did you stay at the Weberstub?'

'Till it closed. That would be about half-past two in the morning.'

'And your wife and Claire were with you from the time they arrived to the time you left?'

'Yes, the whole time. At half-past two we said goodbye to our friends, and the three of us came home together.'

'Which way did you come back?'

'By the Pont Saint-Martin and the Rue des Dentelles, naturally. It was scarcely the moment to go for a walk: as I told you, Edwige was tired, and in a hurry to get to bed.'

'You didn't notice anything unusual by the Dentelles cul-de-sac when you crossed the bridge?'

'I know what you're getting at.' Wotan gave Dullac a sharp look. 'Obviously, Dyana's body was already floating in the river by then. But how could we have possibly imagined it? Besides, it was dark, and the bridge and the inn are relatively distant from the exact spot where the body was found.'

Dullac nodded. 'Yes, I understand. It was too much to hope that you'd be able to give me something definite to go on. I suppose you went straight to bed when you got home?'

'We did. On the first-floor landing I heard my son calling down to me to ask whether Dyana was with us. I told him she wasn't, and we went in; Claire to her room, my wife and I to ours; and we went to sleep. At six o'clock I was woken by your ring at the front door.'

'Thank you. That makes everything perfectly clear,' Dullac said. 'And it's quite apparent from your statement that you've a cast-iron alibi.'

'I'm delighted to hear it,' Wotan said drily and the temperature in the room seemed to drop by several degrees. 'There's one observation I'd like to make, Superintendent. If I had wished to drown my daughter-in-law, I wouldn't have left any marks on her neck. It would be quite out of character for me to do anything so stupid. If you ever do catch the murderer, it'll be entirely due to that blunder.'

'Murderers always do commit them. As you've remarked, there's no such thing as a perfect crime; otherwise, where would we be?'

'Do you want to see my wife now?'

'I was just going to ask you if I might.'

'Very well, I'll call her . . . Oh, by the way, would you mind if I was present at the interview?'

'It's against our usual practice . . . But all right; I've no objection in this case.'

'Now that I'm in the clear, eh?' Wotan said sarcastically; then opened the door and called out in a voice loud enough to bring the walls down, 'Edwige!'

She came in a few moments later and, once again, Holz was struck by the inherent strength of her personality. So many women, in similar circumstances, would have entrenched themselves behind a handkerchief, making no attempt to master their grief. She, on the other hand, appeared erect and impassive, her beautiful, grave Madonna's face turned calmly towards the detectives.

'Please forgive me for bothering you at a time like this,' Dullac said.

'You're doing your duty,' she answered coolly, and

Dullac accepted it as a formal acknowledgement of the obvious; but to Holz it provided confirmation of his previous judgement: she wasn't someone who would be easy to handle.

Dullac sat down again, shifting his chair into a position from which he could keep an eye on Wotan as well as on her. He had a suspicion that the head of the family might influence his wife's answers by imperceptible gestures or looks. But his suspicion was ill-founded. At no time during the interview did Edwige turn her head towards her husband.

'I wanted to ask you to give me an account of your movements on the day of the tragedy,' Dullac began.

'Then it's a murder case you're investigating?' Edwige answered at once in her usual placid tone of voice.

The three men glanced at each other and a fleeting smile of satisfaction appeared on Wotan's face. His wife's intelligence matched his own.

'That is so, isn't it?' she persisted.

Dullac nodded. 'Yes, madame, you're quite right.'

'Otherwise there'd be no point in asking me such questions: they'd be . . . well, let's say, ill-timed.'

'That's so,' Dullac acknowledged. 'Forgive me for not having put you in the picture at once.'

I seem to have been doing the hell of a lot of apologizing since I got here, he thought sourly. Still, his investigation was all that mattered, and if he wanted people to talk he had to be careful not to rub them up the wrong way.

'Regarding my movements on Thursday,' Edwige went on, 'I went shopping in the afternoon in preparation for the meeting in the evening.'

'And what time did your daughter-in-law . . . '

'Dyana wasn't my daughter-in-law,' Edwige inter-rupted. 'Why call her that? Everyone knows Denis and Dyana weren't married. It isn't anything to be ashamed of. Neither of them was particularly anxious to get mar-ried, and whether they did or not was entirely their own affair, after all. So when we're talking about Dyana, I sug-gest we refer to her as Dyana, if you don't mind.'

Dullac was too much taken aback to answer, and she continued, 'It was about six o'clock that I saw Dyana for the last time. My husband and I were in the drawing-room, and she dropped in to have a drink with us.'

'How long did she stay?'

'Only about ten minutes.'

'Did she seem her normal self?'

'Yes, absolutely.'

'What did she talk about?'

'We didn't talk much because the television was on. I think she said something about taking a sleeping pill and having an early night for once. Her job at the cinema was a tiring one.'

'So I understand . . . '

'After she left, I went downstairs with Claire to get the workroom ready for the evening's meeting. At eight o'clock we had dinner.'

'We?'

'Claire, my husband and myself.'

'And then?'

'At half-past eight we went down to receive our guests.'

'Which way do they come in? Do you leave the shop

door open for them?'

'Certainly not! They ring the front-door bell and cross the hall.'

'Do the meetings take place mainly in the shop or in the workroom?'

'We sit in the shop, but the drinks and sandwiches are on a table in the workroom. The communicating door is left wide open, and everyone is free to go from one room to the other to eat or pour themselves a drink or look at Wotan's work.'

'And that was the procedure last Thursday?'

'Yes, exactly.'

'Without anything unusual occurring?'

'Nothing whatever.'

'Wasn't there an argument between your husband and his daughter?'

'There was nothing unusual about that!' For the first time since the interview began, the young woman's face broke into a smile. 'Wotan had rows with Claire, Denis or Dyana twenty times a day! They shout and exchange insults while remaining very fond of each other, and not really meaning a word they say. I'm sure they'd miss their quarrels if they had to give them up. It's their way of showing affection.'

'A sort of game?'

'Yes, that's what it amounts to.'

'Do you mean that your husband and his daughter are merely amusing themselves when they take sides about propagandist art?'

'No, I don't go as far as that. Both of them are quite sincere in their views. But they cease to be when they get worked up about them. That's when the game takes over.'

'I never knew you were such a good psychologist!' Wotan interjected, none too pleased.

Without looking him full in the face, Edwige turned her head slightly and said over her shoulder, 'I'm sorry, darling. But you must admit I'm right.'

'Have it your own way,' Wotan retorted with a surliness that failed to disguise the fact that he found his wife enchanting.

Dullac brought the digression to an end by asking, 'What happened after the argument?'

'Claire went upstairs to see Dyana.'

'How do you know?'

'Because Claire told me so later on.'

'What time was it when she stormed out of the meeting and went up to the second floor?'

'Not very long after everyone got here. So it must have been about nine o'clock.'

'She could have gone up to her own room. So why did she decide to drop in on Dyana?'

'To pour out her annoyance into a sympathetic ear, I imagine.'

'Did they get on well?'

'Oh, very well indeed!' A faint undertone of envy or bitterness seemed to creep into Edwige's voice.

'And you?'

'I don't understand your question.'

'Did you like Dyana?'

After a moment's pause, she asked coldly, 'Do I have to answer that?'

'It would be helpful if you did.'

'Well . . . I appreciated her good qualities.'

'Yes, quite. But did you like her?'

'I've told you that I appreciated her good qualities. That should be sufficient.'

She turned on him a look of such disdain, like that of a queen rebuking an indiscreet subject, that he had not the courage to persist. Instead he asked, 'How long was your stepdaughter out of the room?'

'About an hour. The meeting broke up shortly after she came back.'

'What topics were discussed while she was away?'

'Alchemy, mainly. Some of the younger guests asked my husband to show them the gold leaf used to gild bindings and Wotan took several leaves out of the safe for them to look at. From there, the conversation turned to the Philosopher's Stone and transmutation. Wotan produced some very old books of spells for our friends' benefit, and read out extracts relating to the achievement that alchemists used to dream of: the transformation of lead into gold. And finally, of course, the discussion veered off towards esotericism. And it was at this point that Claire came back again. As a confirmed materialist she felt compelled to take the opposite view to her father's. And, as I was afraid there might be another row, I caught people's eyes and brought the evening to an end.'

'At about half-past ten?'

'Yes. Wotan and his friends left, some of them going on to the Weberstub with him. Claire and I stayed behind to clear away and lock up.'

'Were the gold leaves still lying about in the workroom then?'

'Yes, Wotan forgot to put them back in the safe.'

'Didn't it worry you?'

'Not in the least. In any case, before leaving the house I locked the door between the workroom and the shop. The door's quite strong enough to have reassured us if we'd had the slightest misgiving. Which we didn't.'

'Nothing was stolen from the shop, and the door you're referring to wasn't forced. Yet it provides the only entrance to the workroom. So how do you think the burglars managed to get in?'

'Obviously through the windows; at least, I imagine so.'

'I wanted to ask you about that. How did you leave the windows when you went out?'

'The same as I do every Thursday. I made certain the shutters were secured, but I left the windows open.'

'In spite of it being a cold night?'

'Yes, because the room was thick with cigarette smoke, and my husband can't bear the smell. Our young saleswoman closes the windows as soon as she arrives in the morning, and by the time my husband comes down the room's warmed up again.'

'That means that the saleswoman has a key to the workroom?'

'Yes, she has keys to the shop door, the workroom and the till.'

'And you trust her completely?'

'Yes, of course we do! Florence is the daughter of our friend, Wetzel.'

Dullac looked surprised. 'Ah! I didn't know that. What time was it when you left the house?'

'It would have been shortly after half-past ten. I went to join my husband at the Weberstub.'

'Alone?'

'Yes, alone. Claire wanted to change or pick up a jersey or something. Anyway, she wanted to go up to her room for some reason.'

'Do you think she may have gone up to see Dyana again?'

'She may have. She didn't say she did. You'd better ask her.'

'I will,' Dullac said shortly. 'Did you go straight to the Weberstub?'

'Yes.'

'Which way did you go?'

'Round by the Rue des Moulins.'

'Why by the longer way?'

Edwige hesitated for a moment; then gave a graceful, deprecating shrug, as though acknowledging a weakness. 'Because it's so poetic. I love that street by moonlight; its cobblestones, and all those old houses.'

'Very understandable, madame,' Dullac commented politely.

'I got to the Weberstub before eleven. Claire joined us shortly afterwards.'

'You're positive about that?'

'Absolutely. We had just sat down at a table in the room on the first floor, and from where I was sitting I could see the clock on the wall. When Claire turned up the time on the clock was exactly five past eleven, and I automatically checked it with my watch.' She added immediately, 'I can foresee your next question, and the answer is no. No,

Claire didn't leave us all night till we got home at about half-past two.'

'The three of you walked home together?'

'Yes. I was feeling very tired and took my husband's arm. Claire walked a few steps in front of us.'

'You didn't happen to notice anything unusual when you crossed the Pont Saint-Martin?'

'What could I have noticed? . . . Oh, I see . . . ' Some of the colour left her face. 'No, I didn't see anything, notice anything or imagine anything. How could I have?'

Dullac did not reply and she went on, 'When we got in and went upstairs, my husband's son called down to us: he was worried about Dyana. That was when we heard that she wasn't at home.'

'Weren't you worried, too? And surprised?'

'No, why? Dyana often spent the evening with her friend, Martine, and sometimes stayed very late.'

'Still, it conflicted with what she'd told you at six o'clock: that she intended to stay in and go to bed early. Didn't that occur to you?'

'It wouldn't have been the first time Dyana changed her mind! And I was half-asleep: all I wanted to do was to get to bed. And the puzzle, if one can call it that, didn't strike me as sufficiently interesting for me to want to delve into it.'

Ignoring the irony displayed in her last sentence, Dullac thanked her for her patience in answering his questions, a courtesy she acknowledged with an almost imperceptible nod before leaving the room.

'And now,' Dullac said to Wotan, 'I'd like to talk to your daughter.'

'Easy. I'll go and ask her to join us.'

'Why disturb her? Take me along to her room.'

Wotan did not appear to welcome the suggestion; it seemed as though he suspected it of containing some sinister design on Dullac's part. But, unable to find an excuse, he led the two detectives down the corridor and knocked on Claire's door.

'Can we come in? Superintendent Dullac wants a few words with you.'

The door opened at once, and Dullac took in the scene at a glance. Had he been counting on surprising the young couple in the hope of catching some shade of uneasiness on their faces, he would have been disappointed. There was nothing at all to be read in the untroubled glances with which they met his own.

'Good morning,' he said genially. 'Can I see you for a few minutes?'

'That's a purely rhetorical question,' Claire retorted, quite amiably for her. 'I don't imagine I've any option. Do you know Jacques?' she added, as her father and the detectives came in and sat down in the chairs she casually indicated. She herself returned to the one she appeared to have been occupying when they had knocked, while Jacques remained half-sitting, half-lying on the bed, with one leg tucked under him. Once again, the Superintendent was struck by the young people's innate charm. Nature had certainly been generous to the Grüns and their immediate circle.

The room provided an admirable setting, with its immaculate white walls against which the bright colours of the covers, curtains and cushions stood out vividly.

Through the only window, looking out on the river, the autumnal sun streamed in, investing everything with an air of gaiety, singularly misplaced in the present circumstances.

'So it's turned out to be murder?' Claire said abruptly, unaware that she was opening the conversation in exactly the same way as her stepmother had done half an hour earlier.

'What makes you think so, mademoiselle?' Dullac asked patiently, as he reflected that the women of the family were undoubtedly quick on the uptake.

'Oh, come on! Why else would you be back here today and be ordering – no, forgive me! requesting – Jacques not to leave the house? I presume we're all suspects?'

'There's no reason to be aggressive, mademoiselle. I'm only doing my job. I realize you find being questioned a disagreeable experience, but you should remember that the victim had an infinitely worse one.'

'Nothing can bring Dyana back,' Claire said wearily, but behind the weariness Dullac thought he detected genuine grief.

'I hear you got on very well together.'

She did not reply immediately, and it occurred to him that she must find the presence of her father and young Schiller embarrassing. 'Perhaps you'd prefer to speak to me alone?' he suggested, paying no attention to Wotan's gesture of dissent.

She gave a sigh of relief. 'Yes, I certainly would!'

'But, Claire . . . !' Wotan protested indignantly.

'Please, Father . . . I'd find it much easier.'

Dullac turned to Holz. 'Please wait for me in the office

with Monsieur Grün and Monsieur Schiller. I shan't be
long.'

Slightly surprised, Holz left the room, followed by the
other two men. Dullac moved over to the place on the bed
where Jacques had been sitting. He had always liked
Claire, whose brusque and sometimes insolent manner
concealed, he felt sure, a generous, sensitive and
fundamentally honest nature.

'Now, then?' he said.

Claire took a few seconds to reflect, lit a cigarette and
then exploded, 'They hated her! All of them! I was her
only friend.'

'Oh, come now, mademoiselle,' Dullac said mildly. Her
sudden outburst had startled, even slightly shocked him,
but the last thing he wanted to do was to say anything to
check her now that she seemed about to pour out her heart
to him.

'Oh, for goodness' sake, drop the "mademoiselle",' she
said. 'Everyone calls me Claire, so why don't you do the
same?'

'Just as you like, Claire.'

'You'll think I was exaggerating. All right, they didn't
actually hate her . . . But I understood her, if you see
what I mean?'

'Yes, I know what you mean.'

'She was twenty-five. I'm twenty-three. That inevitably
formed a bond.'

'Your stepmother's twenty-five, too,' Dullac pointed
out.

'Exactly!'

She had put so much vigour and so many innuendoes

into her 'exactly' that Dullac pricked up his ears. 'Do you
mean . . . '

'I mean that at twenty-five, Edwige behaves like a terribly respectable middle-aged woman. I suppose in a way
she has to. After all, she's Wotan Grün's wife, and in
Strasbourg that's quite something. But if it wasn't for the
position she has to live up to there'd be nothing to stop us
looking on her as one of us, as a real friend.'

'But she doesn't want to be?'

'No. Rather than descend from her pedestal she deliberately killed the young girl who must have been fighting to
get out. Haven't you taken a good look at her? She's a
corpse.'

'You're a bit severe on her, aren't you?'

'A corpse. And Dyana . . . Dyana was so radiantly
alive! That's why Edwige envied her. Because Dyana was
free! And she envies me, too, for the same reason.'

'Granted that's so, why are you telling me all this?'

'Because their hypocrisy makes me sick. Denis will certainly grieve, grieve a lot and have great difficulty in getting over it. Because Dyana was his mother. Do you
understand? His *mother*! Denis has never grown up. He's
got a brain all right. He's an intellectual. But he won't
accept any responsibility. He was only six when our
mother died: I suppose that gives him some sort of excuse.
Dyana wanted a man to share her life with, not a child. If
only he'd pull himself together! He's got the looks and
physique to make a woman happy, so why does he go
round with that idiotic little beard, spectacles and round
shoulders? He's two years younger than I am, but anyone
would think he was at least five years older.'

This was perfectly true, Dullac reflected, but before he could make any comment Claire was off again. It didn't look as if anything could stop her now she had started.

'That's why Dyana must have wanted him to marry her. Because then their roles would have been clearly defined. But no! Denis was perfectly happy to leave things as they were. He was afraid that once he was legally married to Dyana everyone would expect him to assume the responsibilities of a husband. And he found the life he'd been living with her for the last four years much more attractive. Of the two of them it was she who was really the man. Admittedly, the grant Denis received from the university played the predominant part in balancing their budget; but, all the same, it was Dyana who left the house each day to go to work, and it was Dyana who was paid a salary at the end of each month.'

'But, Claire,' Dullac broke in, 'I always thought you were pro Women's Lib?'

'Women's Lib never meant that women should sweat blood and tears to earn enough money to feed their boy-friends! And there's something else . . . '

'What?' Dullac murmured in a slight daze, wondering what revelation could be coming next.

'It's rather a delicate subject. In a way, Denis scarcely fulfilled the part one expects a man to play during the daytime. But, if what Dyana told me was true, he wasn't any better at night.'

'You mean he was impotent?' Dullac asked, surprised.

'No, certainly not. But . . . I scarcely know how to put it . . . there were apparently moments when Dyana would have preferred him to be rather less restrained and respectful. In bed, like everywhere else, my brother behaved more like a child than an adult. Still, Dyana was very much in love with him, and I know he felt the same about her. I often tried to get him to wake up, and I longed for the day when he got his degree, because I thought that would bring about a change in his outlook. I waited and hoped. And then this happened! What's there to hope and wait for now? Everything's over for poor Dyana.'

'But not for your brother,' Dullac said sympathetically. 'It must have been a tremendous shock for him. Maybe when he gets over it you'll find he's a different person: much more mature and responsible.'

'You're kind,' Claire said with a note of such naïve surprise in her voice that it made Dullac smile.

'You didn't think a detective could be kind?'

She brushed the question aside with an evasive gesture. 'Well, that's that. I've shot my mouth off, as they say. You didn't even have to twist my arm.'

'I'm grateful to you for trusting me. I need scarcely say that I'll keep everything you've told me to myself and only make use of it in so far as it helps with my inquiries. There's one more thing you can do for me: tell me how you spent your time on the night of the crime.'

'You don't have to bother with that,' Claire said airily. 'I promise you I've a perfect alibi!'

'It's not just a question of an alibi. Your statement will enable me to check other people's and it may eventually put me on the right track.'

Claire paused for a moment to collect her thoughts. Her cigarette had now burnt to the end and she stubbed it out in an ashtray with one of those firm, precise gestures that he found so attractive in her, and so reminiscent of her father.

The details that followed tallied exactly with those he had received from Wotan and Edwige. The discussion group had met at half-past eight, and shortly afterwards she had got into an argument with her father which had become so embittered that she had gone up to Dyana at about nine o'clock to cool down. She had found her in her pyjamas and dressing-gown, preparing to go to bed. For an hour or so the two of them had chatted about this and that over a drink. Then, at about ten o'clock, Claire and Dyana had parted on the second-floor landing, and, while Dyana had presumably gone to bed, Claire had returned to the meeting.

In reply to a question from Dullac, she told him, 'Yes, I thought Dyana was her normal self. She seemed to be tired by her job and a bit concerned, as usual, about Denis; but apart from that she didn't seem to have any worries of any kind.'

Shortly after Claire had returned to the meeting on the ground floor, Edwige had brought the proceedings to an end. Then, when the guests had left, Claire had helped her tidy up the room: this had taken about a quarter of an hour.

'Then the two of you went off to the Weberstub?' Dullac inquired smoothly.

Claire gave him a reproachful glance. 'Now, it isn't kind of you, Superintendent, to lay a trap for me. My father and stepmother must have told you – and you can't have forgotten – that I left Edwige at that particular moment and went up to the flat.'

'You're quite right, Claire, I hadn't forgotten. Did you want to fetch something from your bedroom?'

'No. I wanted to telephone Jacques.'

Dullac's eyebrows rose. 'At eleven o'clock at night?'

'Jacques wasn't in Strasbourg that night,' Claire said calmly, looking him straight in the face. 'He was in Colmar, staying with a friend of his, and we'd arranged that I'd call him late in the evening.' She added, smiling, 'Since we became friends, Jacques has adopted the habits of the Grün clan: he's become a night-bird.'

'Would you mind telling me the purpose of the call?'

'There wasn't one. As we weren't going to see each other for forty-eight hours we both just thought it would be nice to have a little chat.'

Dullac nodded. 'I see.'

'What do you see?' Claire demanded with some of her former aggressiveness.

'I see you're very much in love,' Dullac explained. Almost as he spoke, he realized that he had allowed a faint note of bitterness to creep into his voice and silently cursed himself for his idiocy. Reverting quickly to his professional role, he asked, 'How long did your conversation last?'

'I don't really remember. Ten minutes, perhaps, or possibly a bit more. Anyway, as soon as I hung up I collected a sweater from my bedroom and went straight to the Weberstub, which I got to round about eleven.'

'Which way did you go?'

'The shortest one. I told you I went straight there.'

'You mean, by the Rue des Dentelles and the Pont Saint-Martin?'

'Yes, obviously.'

'And from eleven o'clock in the evening till half-past two in the morning, when your family and you left the Weberstub, none of you got up from the table?'

'No, none of us at any time.'

'And you got back to the house at the same time as your father and stepmother?'

'Yes. When we got up to our landing my brother called down to us. It seemed to me that he hadn't come out of his own flat but from his neighbour's – one of your former colleagues, Superintendent.'

'What did Denis say?'

'He wanted to know if Dyana was with us.'

'Did you go to bed immediately afterwards?'

'Yes, at once. It had been rather a tempestuous evening! And it was late. All three of us were in a hurry to get to sleep.' She added with a glint of amusement, 'Now is there anything else you can possibly think of to ask me, Superintendent?'

'Not at the moment, but perhaps we can have another talk later on?'

'I'll look forward to it,' she assured him.

He left her and returned to the office, where he found Holz waiting with Wotan and Schiller.

'Your turn next!' he said to the young man with rather forced cheerfulness.

Jacques responded with a comic grimace of alarm, which he found rather likeable.

Before getting down to business, Dullac turned to Wotan. 'Forgive me,' he said, 'but, as you know, I prefer to conduct my inquiries in private. So I'd like to see Monsieur Schiller alone.'

'Just as you wish,' Jacques broke in, 'but my life's as pure as the driven snow, so I shan't be in the least embarrassed if Wotan stays.'

'Possibly not, but I still prefer to do it my way,' Dullac insisted.

At this point, Wotan looked at his watch and announced that it was high time he went downstairs and got to work on his bindings, thereby giving the impression that he was leaving the room of his own free will.

Dullac addressed Holz. 'Go down to the shop with our friend and have a talk with Mademoiselle Florence. Get her to tell you her story and ask her where and when I can meet her father.'

'Old Wetzel?'

'Yes, old Wetzel who's a member of the discussion group. Old Wetzel, who was in Gräber's bar next to Madame Dickbauch on the night of the crime. Old Wetzel, whose daughter works as a salesgirl in the Grün shop. And, now I come to think of it, as you've got the list of the members of the discussion group on you, ask Grün to put a tick against the names of those who were with him at the Weberstub on the night of Thursday/Friday. That way we'll find out if old Wetzel was one of them. Come back here in half an hour and we'll go up and see Denis Grün.'

Holz saluted and went out, leaving Dullac alone with Jacques Schiller.

The latter said pleasantly, 'You know I've really nothing to hide.'

'From me?'

'Well, yes, you too. But I really meant from Wotan. If

he thinks he's got anything to complain of, I couldn't care less!'

Dullac smiled. 'I gather you're not on the friendliest terms?'

'I wouldn't say that. Actually, I like him. He gives a damn good impersonation of a Rabelaisian patriarch, and as I enjoy the theatre . . . '

' . . . His performance amuses you,' Dullac finished for him.

'Up to a point. But what's behind it all?'

'Behind?'

'Yes. Behind Grün the clown there's the man. What sort of man is it?'

'You've got me interested,' Dullac said. 'What's your opinion?'

'A kid! A big spoilt child, a big sulky baby, seasoned with a lot of egotism, and an iron will that could make you giddy.'

'You seem to be a very shrewd psychologist.'

'Kind of you to say so! As a matter of fact, I'm aiming to get a degree in philosophy. I'm in my first year at the university.' He caught sight of Dullac's expression and asked, 'What's so surprising about that?'

'Something Wotan said to me.'

'What?'

'He said it kindly, mind you, but he seemed convinced that you hadn't any prospects.'

'Yes, I know. He regards philosophy as a useless luxury. It goes to show how contrary human beings can be. There's a man who's literate and aesthetic to his finger-tips, yet he wants all the young men with whom he comes in contact to take up engineering! To him, all philosophy can lead to is a professorship.'

'Perhaps Wotan expects rather more from you because he sees you as his future son-in-law.'

'I haven't the least idea whether Claire and I will get married. In any case, we aren't planning to do so in the immediate future.'

'I don't want to be indiscreet, but do you find your relationship with Claire entirely satisfactory? Isn't she inclined to be . . . well, rather bossy?'

Jacques laughed. 'You seem to share Wotan's views. He believes man should command and woman obey. He's quite unaware that, for all her docile manner, Edwige can twist him round her little finger. What I like about Claire is that she regards the two of us as being on an equal footing. And if she happens to give me an order I may happen to want to obey it.'

'You wouldn't mind becoming her slave?'

After a moment's reflection, Jacques gave a good-humoured shrug. 'You know, I think I see myself more as her page.'

Dullac was conscious of a pang of regret. Scarcely fifteen years separated him from this boy, only twelve from Claire, yet there seemed no vestige of his own youth left. When had it forsaken him? His thoughts switched abruptly to Edwige, and he felt a sudden sympathy for her: she, too, had sacrificed her youth in order to maintain her position with appropriate dignity. Though he did, in fact, share Wotan's views on the roles of men and women when they were in love, he could find nothing to disapprove of in Jacques's and Claire's reciprocal sentiments.

Theirs was a different way of loving, that was all.

Pulling himself together, he observed, 'In short, your relationship is rather like that between Dyana and Denis?'

'Yes, perhaps. But I think Dyana wanted Denis to be . . . '

'More self-assertive?'

'No, not that, because she was very independent. But she would have liked him to be more self-confident, more adult in his outlook. There were moments when she felt cheated, almost exploited. While Denis spent his evenings very comfortably at home discussing revolution with his friend Charles, Dyana was slaving away at the Lorelei to earn their keep. And *he* looked down on *her*! That really was too much!'

'Yes, I quite agree. You liked her very much, didn't you?'

'Enormously!' Jacques's answer came without a moment's hesitation.

'How about Madame Grün?'

'Oh, Edwige is all right. Always very nice to me.'

'But you're less enthusiastic about her?'

'Well, there's a great difference, isn't there? When I think of Claire or Dyana or Martine, I think of them as girls. But I think of Edwige as a woman. One can picture Claire or Martine putting their feet up on the table: with Edwige, it would be impossible.'

'Claire told me that you were in Colmar on Thursday night.'

'Yes, staying with a friend.'

'What's his name?'

'Roland Berthet. I'll give you his address if you like.'

Jacques bent over the desk, scribbled on a loose sheet of paper and handed it to Dullac. 'There you are! You can ask him: he'll confirm it.'

'I can't really see what motive you could have had for killing Dyana,' Dullac admitted. 'It's just a matter of routine.'

'Yes, I understand.'

'What time did Claire ring you up?'

'We'd arranged that she'd call me somewhere around eleven. It must have been ten to.'

'That tallies.'

'Yes, but it doesn't prove anything.'

'Why not?'

'Because Claire and I could easily have cooked up the story when we were alone in her bedroom a short while ago.'

Dullac burst out laughing. 'Well, you've certainly got a nerve!'

'I didn't mean to be impertinent.'

'I believe you . . . But as you've pointed out, the evidence of your friend in Colmar will carry more weight than Claire's. I suspect she's very much in love with you and would be prepared to lie shamelessly to keep you out of trouble.'

'She's a Grün!' Jacques said by way of ending the conversation.

3

As he left the flat, Dullac bumped into Holz, who had come up from the workroom.

'Mission accomplished!' the Inspector announced. 'As far as young Florence is concerned, she's a member of the discussion group, like her father, and their names are on the list. She confirms the accounts the Grüns gave us of the meeting and the times. Neither she nor her father went on to the Weberstub with the Grüns on the night in question. And you'll have no difficulty in meeting her father as he spends every day at his gallery in the Rue de la Mésange.'

'Close to Headquarters. Very convenient.'

'I also asked Grün to mark the list in the way you wanted. It wasn't one he'd specially made out for our benefit as I'd thought at first: it was just an ordinary typed list of the regular members.'

Dullac took the list from him and ran through it, as he had not had the chance to do so earlier, in Wotan's presence.

'I see two of the names have been crossed out,' he observed a moment later.

They were those of the Protestant clergyman, Robert Michelon, and his wife.

'Did he tell you why?'

Holz shook his head. 'No, and I didn't like to bother him. All he did was to tick the names of the people who were at the Weberstub on Thursday.'

There were fifteen names on the list:-

Wotan Grün. (Web.)
Edwige Grün. (Web.)
Claire Grün. (Web.)
Florent Wetzel.
Florence Wetzel.
Pastor Robert Michelon. (name crossed out)
Madame Robert Michelon. (name crossed out)
Father Dominique Doppelleben.
Wilfrid-Hamlet Boersen. (Web.)
Alice Reine-Camyon de Potztausend. (Web.)
Daniel Schwarz.
Gilbert Gruau. (Web.)
Janine Gruau. (Web.)
Germain Andros.
Abigail Andros.

'Well, it gives us something to work on,' Dullac
remarked. 'We'll ask Wotan later on to tell us a bit about
them and give us their addresses. And at the same time
we'll ask him why the Pastor and his wife have been
removed from the list.'

'In any case,' Holz said, 'there were four people with
Grün at the Weberstub besides his wife and daughter.
Boersen, the two Gruaus, and that Alice somebody-or-
other. So his alibi certainly seems to be watertight unless
all four of them turn out to be liars, or he's found a way to
be in two places at once.'

'Both equally unlikely,' Dullac commented. 'I can't see
Grün being able to bribe those four witnesses. I've met the
Gruaus once or twice: they're two young psychiatrists,
typical of their profession. Madame de Potztausend is an

eccentric, well known among the intelligentsia of Strasbourg: she's a wealthy widow, a poetess and a pain in the neck! She collared me one evening in the Rue de la Nuée Bleue as I was leaving my office; said someone had stolen her peke. I could only get rid of her, after she'd wasted an hour of my time, by promising to take charge of the case myself. Later the same evening, she rang me up to say she'd found her poor little doggie locked up by mistake in the wine cellar. And next morning I received an old-fashioned tantalus accompanied by a letter of apology that read suspiciously like a proposal.'

'I suppose it is about time you thought of getting married, Chief,' Holz suggested earnestly.

'Very possibly, but not with Alice Reine-Camyon de Potztausend. That's a punishment I wouldn't wish on anyone, not even Dyana Pasquier's murderer!'

Dullac led the way up to the second floor and rang the bell on his right. Music filtered out from behind the door.

'Wagner!' Dullac pronounced. 'Young Denis seems to be drowning his sorrow in *Rheingold*.'

Though he had only rung the one bell, the doors to right and left opened simultaneously: Denis appeared on the threshold of one; Noel Loiseau, the retired police officer, on the threshold of the other.

The latter said apologetically, 'Oh, I'm so sorry, I thought . . . ' then recognized the Superintendent. 'Dullac! I was so glad to hear you'd been put in charge of this distressing affair.'

'How are you?' Dullac inquired amiably and introduced Holz.

The two of them shook hands and Loiseau continued,

'Very kind of you to ask after my health, my dear Dullac. I can't say I'm as well as I'd like to be. Not that it's anything serious. Just arthritis. It won't stop me living to a hundred, but I'm afraid I'll have a painful journey getting there.'

Dullac nodded sympathetically and turned to Denis. 'I'd like to have a few words with you.'

'Would anyone mind if I joined you?' Loiseau asked eagerly. 'I feel my presence would be comforting to my young friend here and . . . well, it'd remind me of the good old days!'

Dullac raised no objection – Loiseau was very popular with his former colleagues – and the four men moved into the flat which for the last three years had been Dyana Pasquier's home. The living-room was separated from the bedroom by a wide double curtain, which today was drawn back. It revealed a low bed and, above it, a large portrait of a young woman between twenty and twenty-five, painted by a certain Daniel Schwarz, whose name seemed vaguely familiar to Dullac, though for the moment he could not recall where he had heard it.

It was a half-length portrait, and depicted the sitter in a white blouse with a broad open collar, as she might have appeared to Lautrec. Beauty, and – even more so – charm could not have been better captured than they were in her face, with the perfect flesh tints, neither too pale nor too ochred, and the small, well-drawn mouth, half-open, not so much in a smile as an expression of surprise, or perhaps gentle mockery. But most attractive of all were the eyes and the look, in which could be read a whole range of qualities at first sight contradictory; dreaminess and

crystal clarity, energy and romantic languor. And over-
lying everything was a mockery, responding to that of the
mouth, a gay mockery in which there was no shadow of
unkindness. It was Dyana Pasquier as she had been when
death came to reap her in her twenty-sixth year.

As soon as his guests had settled down on the low chairs
and cushions scattered about the room, Denis headed for
the stereo alongside his radio and tape-recorder, and took
off the record to which he had been listening when inter-
rupted by the detectives' visit. With slow, meticulous gestures, in contrast to those of his father and sister, which
could often be violent, he returned the record to its sleeve
and replaced the sleeve in a rack. Dullac had not been
mistaken: it had been *Rheingold* all right.

'Music can be a great consolation when we're
unhappy,' Loiseau observed sententiously.

Showing no signs of having heard him, Denis sat down
on a pouffe with his crossed hands gripped between his
knees, and placidly surveyed his visitors with eyes wholly
void of expression.

Embarrassed, Dullac managed to utter a few words of
condolence, which Denis dismissed with a wave of his
hand.

'Thank you. I know it's kindly meant, but there's
nothing anyone can say that will help at the moment.'

The interview threatened to be painful, and, anxious to
cut it as short as possible, Dullac came swiftly to the point
and asked him how he had spent the evening and night of
the previous Thursday.

'I spent the evening with my friend, Charles Feldmann,
at his room in the Rue Gutenberg,' Denis answered and

went no further. As the other three men remained silent, too, he eventually felt compelled to go on, though it obviously required a considerable effort.

'I got there about seven o'clock: he'd invited me to dinner. After dinner we talked for quite a time: it must have been about ten o'clock when I left. He walked back with me and we talked for a minute or so more outside the house. We could hear my father's discussion group still in full swing, so there was no fear of anyone coming out and interrupting us.'

'Did you never think of taking part in those discussions yourself?' Dullac asked innocently.

The question produced such an expression of horror on the young man's face that, in happier circumstances, Dullac would have burst out laughing.

'No, it never occurred to Charles or me to do anything like that,' Denis declared.

'In that case he could have gone up with you to your flat.'

Denis shook his head. 'No, because Dyana had told me she intended to go to bed early, and we didn't want to disturb her.'

'So you said goodbye to your friend outside the house, and came straight up here?'

'Yes, that's right. I had taken the door-key with me so as to get in without waking Dyana. Before going in I rang Monsieur Loiseau's bell, because I had a splitting headache, and remembered noticing that morning that we were out of aspirin.'

'That's quite correct,' Loiseau confirmed. 'I can even add that it was exactly a quarter past ten. I never go to bed early and Denis often drops in to have a chat with me.'

'Is that what happened last Thursday?' Dullac asked.

'No,' Denis answered. 'I told you I had a headache. I just borrowed a couple of tablets from Monsieur Loiseau and went straight to my own flat. I was undressing as quietly as I could with one small light on so as not to disturb Dyana but just then she woke up all the same. She asked me to tell her about my evening with Charles and what we'd talked about. She wasn't being malicious, I'm quite certain of that: just the opposite. She wanted to show genuine interest in my doings, because for some time our lives had been running on parallel lines; that's to say, they scarcely seemed to meet any more. Unfortunately, the conversation that had started perfectly pleasantly degenerated into an argument. It wasn't the first of its kind. I ought to have been on my guard, because the topics Charles and I most enjoyed discussing weren't the sort that Dyana could listen to without flying into a temper. But how could I have guessed what would follow? Dyana's temper led to a flood of complaints; everything that had been building up for months finally came out. I was all the more upset because there was quite a lot of truth in her accusations. Finally she got up, got dressed again and left, slamming the door behind her . . . And that was the last I was to see of her,' Denis added. Though his voice had not faltered and there had been nothing emotive in his choice of words, his distress was clearly apparent.

He lapsed into silence for some little time and none of the other three felt disposed to intrude on it. At length, he went on, 'I was terribly shaken by our quarrel and went

across to my friend Loiseau's flat, where I poured out all
my troubles to him until I heard voices below; my family
had come back from the Weberstub. I opened Loiseau's
door and asked my father whether, as I'd hoped, Dyana
had joined them, but she hadn't. So then I assumed that,
to teach me a lesson, she'd gone round to her friend Martine's, and wouldn't be coming back till daybreak. As it
was already very late, I left Loiseau and went back to my
own flat. But I couldn't sleep; I didn't even attempt to. I
tried to read, but I found it impossible to concentrate: all I
could do was chain-smoke. And that's how you found me
when you came up here with my father at six o'clock in the
morning.'

'Thank you,' Dullac said. 'I realize how painful it must
have been for you to go into all these details, but I'm sure
you understand that they're indispensable if we're to get
at the truth. There are just two further details relating to
times that I hope you'll be able to remember exactly: what
time was it when Mademoiselle Pasquier left here, and
you rang our friend Loiseau's bell? And secondly, what
time was it when you left him?'

It was Loiseau who answered. 'I can tell you that
myself. I was reading in my living-room when I first heard
the sound of raised voices. Old professional habits are
ingrained, and I automatically looked at the time. It was
twenty to eleven, or, if you prefer it, twenty-two hours
forty. Shortly afterwards I heard Dyana open her front
door, and, as I was very fond of the young couple, I
opened mine with the intention of pouring oil on the
troubled waters. But I was too late; Dyana was in such a
rage she didn't see or hear me; she rushed downstairs and

remained deaf to my and Denis's pleas to her to come back. It was then, seeing how miserable he was, that I invited Denis into my flat. We talked for a long time. He told me all about his life with Dyana during the four years they had been together; their hopes, their early struggles, followed recently by disagreements and difficulties which in Denis's eyes spelt the imminent break-up of their relationship, but in mine seemed no more than the small snags which young couples inevitably encounter when the first rapture is over. In other words, being three times as old as the young people, I didn't consider the situation to be nearly as serious as Denis made it out to be. And I tried to bring him round to my view. But he always came back to the same point: his only hope of retaining Dyana's affection was to marry her, and he could not contemplate doing that until he had got his degree and a teaching job. He insisted on showing me a letter Dyana had written him some months before. In order to express her point of view more clearly without becoming involved in a quarrel, the young woman had set out in black and white not her grievances, but her analysis of the causes of their growing estrangement. Denis saw in this document – which he had carefully kept – one more reason to give up hope; I, on the other hand, saw in it proof, had I needed it, that Dyana was an intelligent, reasonable young woman, and it seemed to augur well for their future.

'Regarding your second question, I imagine that the Grüns have already answered it. My watch and my clock both showed the time to be half-past two when we heard Wotan, Edwige and Claire come back from the Weber-stub. Denis leant over the banister and asked if Dyana was with them. When they said she wasn't it seemed to depress him still more. I told him, rather sharply this time, not to make mountains out of molehills, hoping that it would make him pull himself together. He promised me he'd try to stop worrying, and we said goodnight. He went back to his flat, and I returned to mine, pretty exhausted, I must admit, and went straight to bed.'

Dullac felt pretty exhausted, too, after this dissertation, but he was careful to conceal it. As he got to his feet, he said, 'I'm very grateful to you both for all the information. It's been of considerable help.' Then, addressing Loiseau, he asked, 'May we come back with you to your flat for a minute or two?'

'Yes, of course. Delighted!'

Denis had already returned to the consolation of Wagner as the three police officers crossed the landing and settled down in Loiseau's neat little studio flat to talk things over.

Dullac began by remarking to him, 'I imagine you're on pretty intimate terms with the whole family?'

'Intimate would be overstating it,' Loiseau answered. 'The Grüns lease me this studio, and I maintain a good neighbourly relationship with them. I wouldn't put it more strongly than that.'

'Would you mind giving me your rough impression of each of them?'

'They'll be the same as yours! One doesn't have to be very perceptive or to have known them for a long time to make up one's mind about them. Wotan dominates the whole family from his great height, both physically and mentally. He's a splendid, genuine sort of character, an artist with real creative gifts. He's inclined to be dictatorial, but in a good-humoured way: I suppose you might call it the iron hand in the velvet glove. The less attractive facets of his character are his egotism and a slight streak of megalomania.'

'What do you suppose Edwige's real motives were in marrying him?'

'It's perfectly possible that she married him because she was in love with him. I hope that was the case. Because if she married him for his money she was foolish; a cage remains a cage even when it's gilded. And a young woman of twenty-five, if she's reasonably adult, often thrives better in an attic than a palace.'

'Your view corresponds almost exactly with Claire's.'

'Ah, Claire! She couldn't be more different! The spitting image of her father, physically and mentally.'

'And a very pretty girl, too.'

'You've noticed that, have you?' There was a twinkle in the glance that Loiseau shot at the Superintendent before he went on, 'That just leaves the brother. He's a Grün, too, whatever his father may think of him. He's got his pride and a fair dose of talent. Not at all a bad chap.'

Holz and Dullac took a moment or two to digest the older man's impressions. Finally, Dullac asked abruptly, 'Then which one was it?'

Taken aback, Loiseau played for time by pretending not to understand the question. 'Which one was what?'

'Which one killed her?'

After a short silence spent in collecting his thoughts, Loiseau observed, 'These things depend on the view-point one adopts. One can study the problem from a psycholog-

ical angle or one can seek to make deductions from the
alibis. I've learnt from experience that when the
psychology and the alibis point in the same direction, one
isn't far from one's goal. In the present context, from what
I know of them, I can assure you that neither Wotan
Grün, nor his wife, nor Jacques, nor Claire, nor of course
Denis seem to me to have had any reason whatever to have
wished for Dyana's death. So what about the alibis?'

Dullac heaved a sigh. 'I haven't checked them yet, but
at first sight they appear quite unassailable. How do you
feel about the famous discussion group?'

Loiseau gave a short laugh. 'I was waiting for you to
come to them! They're all good friends of Wotan, which
means that each of them thoroughly dislikes him and is
jealous of his success.'

'In that case,' Dullac said, 'we'd better get cracking and
tackle them.'

4

Dullac looked around when they were out on the landing
and remarked, 'I don't see the stairs up to the loft.'

'That's because they're collapsible,' Loiseau explained.
'If you watch the trap-door over your head, I'll show you
the mechanism.'

He gripped a handle set into the wall and pulled it. The
trap-door then swung up and a sectional ladder appeared
from the open space and slid down to their feet.

'Let's go up and have a look round,' Dullac suggested.
'You never know.'

The three of them climbed up and found themselves in a vast room under the roof which extended over the whole area of the Grün house. A certain amount of order prevailed: old cupboards, packing-cases and cardboard boxes standing against the walls had enabled some sort of classification to be made of all the traditional junk customarily stored away in lofts. A number of dresses and theatrical costumes hanging from a rod in one corner had been made by Claire for her cabaret shows and stored there to prevent them from cluttering up her Paris flat; in another corner there was a child's see-saw; beside it lay a pile of dumb-bells, chest-expanders and other tackle, the remaining traces of Wotan's athletic youth. Secured by a nail, the portrait of Grandfather Grün dominated the whole loft, which was lighted by narrow windows with relatively clean panes sunk into the four walls.

Suddenly, Holz, who was standing close to one of them, called out, 'Hey! Come and look at this!'

The other two hurried over only to find him admiring the view.

'Holz!' Dullac snapped at him, displeased.

'Don't tick him off,' Loiseau said indulgently. 'He's quite right to admire it. Take a look yourself.'

And the view over the whole of Strasbourg under the clear blue morning sky certainly was magnificent. Dullac allowed himself a few moments to take it in before going down again to face his daily round with its violence and horror, much as an exhausted diver regains the surface to gulp in lungfuls of fresh air before disappearing again beneath the troubled waters.

'Well?' Loiseau broke in. 'What do you think of it?

Worth the climb, wasn't it?'

The word 'climb' brought the detectives back to a sense of duty. They had not come up there as tourists but to pry into the Grüns' private lives. In the end, they failed to discover anything of interest in the cupboards, drawers and wooden cases they rummaged through, but Dullac was not unduly disappointed: he had scarcely expected the loft to play any part in the affair.

The three of them returned to the landing where Holz, intrigued by the trap-door's mechanism, asked Loiseau, 'How do you shut it again?'

'You give the ladder a push. The counterpoise does the rest of the work for you.'

He applied the upward pressure and the heavy ladder retracted into the loft, as the trap-door closed over the vacant space.

5

Loiseau returned to his flat and the two detectives went downstairs to the ground floor. As Holz headed for the front door, Dullac called him back.

'I want to see Grün about that list,' he reminded him, and entered the shop through the door on his right. Florence gave him a pleasant smile as, followed by Holz, he crossed the room and knocked on the communicating door.

Wotan roared out, 'Come in!'; then, when he caught sight of Dullac, exclaimed half-jokingly, half-irritably, 'What, you again!'

Dullac explained the reason for his visit and Wotan remarked more amiably, 'In short, what you want is a portrait gallery? Very well, let's get on with it.'

He took the list that Dullac held out to him and rattled off, 'My wife, my daughter and me! I hope I can dispense with any comments there? Wetzel. Florence's father. Pleasant fellow. Round about fifty. Owner of the Wetzel Art Gallery in the Rue de la Mésange. I exhibited a very fine sixteenth-century lectern there that I'd picked up in Germany, and Wetzel sold it for me: in return I sold a number of antiques for him. He's a widower. Florence is his only child. When Dyana refused the post of salesgirl that I offered her, Florence happened to be looking for a job. Rather than take on a complete stranger – after all, I've got some very valuable things in my shop! – I was only too happy to put the daughter of an old friend in charge.'

'But the Wetzels don't live in the Rue de la Mésange, do they?' Dullac asked, remembering that Wetzel had been one of the group surrounding Madame Dickbauch on the night of the crime.

'No, they live in the Rue du Pont Saint-Martin, just opposite the Protestant Church.'

Seizing the opportunity, Dullac said, 'Talking of the Protestant Church, I noticed that the names of the Pastor and his wife had been struck off your list.'

Wotan suddenly looked embarrassed, a very rare occurrence for him. 'Oh, it was just a trifling matter; a small difference of opinion over how the discussion group should be run. I never took it seriously but the poor Michelons did: they decided to resign.'

'What was the difference of opinion about?'

'Nothing of importance, as I told you. Michelon and a few others took exception to the Grüns having so much influence. But as the discussion group was formed ten years ago at my suggestion, what could be more natural than for my house and me to be its centre? Some people didn't like the arrangement and proposed that the meetings be held at the various members' houses in rotation. Now, how could I be expected to agree to that?'

As Dullac did not answer, he went on, 'I was magnanimous about it, and all the dissenters eventually withdrew their objections and continued to come here, except for the Pastor, who stubbornly refused to. Just a question of his pride being hurt, that was all.'

'Well, that explains that. Let's move on. What about Father Dominique Doppelleben?'

'Professor of Theology at the university. Very cultured. Very likeable, too. He was one of those who refused to support the Pastor and his friends.'

'Wilfrid-Hamlet Boersen?'

'An extremely clever young man. Shows great promise. His father is Danish consul at the Council of Europe.'

'How old is he?'

'Fifty and a bit.'

'No, the son?'

'Ah, him. Twenty-three. Well-educated, aesthetic, has very good taste. He admires my work. Admires me, too, for that matter.'

'I see he went to the Weberstub with you on Thursday evening.'

'Yes, he loves to hear me talk.'

'You needn't bother with Madame de Potztausend, I know her . . . '

'Thorough old nuisance!' Wotan exploded. 'She wanted me to do a binding for her poems! What next! Who ever heard of imitation jewellery being put in a velvet case? Her poems! . . . '

'You don't think much of them?'

'Oh, most of them scan all right, I'll admit that,' Wotan said with a burst of his Homeric laughter.

Dullac smiled. 'That tells me enough. What about Daniel Schwarz?'

Wotan gave a contemptuous snort. 'A nonentity. Poor as a church mouse. Lives in Ingwiller, thirty kilometres north of here. Twenty years old. Not bad-looking.'

'What's he do?'

'Paints.'

'Yes, of course.' Dullac suddenly remembered. 'He did the portrait of Dyana that hangs in your son's bedroom.'

'Yes, that's his. He was a friend of Dyana's.'

'We can skip the Gruaus. I know them. That just leaves the Androses. I seem to know the name . . . '

'They aren't a married couple; they're a father and daughter. Germain Andros is director of the Comédie du Rhin, our leading regional theatre.'

'And his daughter?'

'A nice girl. About twenty. Almost certainly a virgin. Blushes whenever Daniel shows up. Makes herself useful by typing the minutes of our meetings.'

'I see,' Dullac said, though there had not been much for him to see so far.

'Are you proposing to call on all of these people,

Superintendent?'

'I'll have to. You don't seem to fancy the idea,' Dullac added after noticing Wotan's expression.

'It's all one to me. I'll let you have their addresses right away . . . And good luck to you! I'm glad it's your job and not mine.'

'I rather guessed that,' the Superintendent murmured under his breath.

MONDAY

1

Next day was Sunday. Dullac spent it at his flat in the Rue Paul-Janet, sprawled in an armchair, eating next to nothing, chain-smoking and concentrating on the case.

On Monday morning he picked up Holz at Police Headquarters, and they set off to call on the members of the discussion group. As the Wetzel Art Gallery was only a stone's throw away they went there first.

Wetzel took obvious pleasure in showing them round the oil paintings and various antiques on display, which reflected his good taste and his cunning eye for what should prove saleable. But the time came when Dullac felt constrained to tell him that he and Holz were not there as art-lovers but in their professional capacity.

'So there's no doubt about it, she was murdered,' Wetzel murmured. 'It's appalling! One wonders how such things can happen. A prowler, I suppose. Had she been assaulted?'

'Apparently,' Dullac said drily, 'since she's dead.'

'Yes, quite . . . But what I really meant . . . '

'Ah, I see. No, she hadn't been assaulted in the way you mean.'

'Then she must have disturbed the burglars while they were on the job.'

'It's possible, but once they'd completed it, why would

they go to the trouble of fishing the body out of the river again and dumping it in the workroom?'

'Yes, why indeed?' Wetzel muttered, bemused. 'The whole thing's quite baffling. And what a sad loss for my friends, the Grüns! When Madame Dickbauch's screams woke me up that night, I thought I recognized the body as Dyana's the moment I saw it. I hoped I might be wrong, but . . . well, I wasn't. I don't know how Denis will ever get over it.'

'You think he loved her as much as all that?'

'Are you joking, Superintendent?'

'I'm asking. Apparently they were constantly having rows.'

Wetzel spread out his arms in a gesture of anger. 'What does that prove? My dear wife and I quarrelled for twenty-five years and I still miss her dreadfully. If it weren't for Florence . . . '

'Was your daughter a close friend of Dyana's?'

'I wouldn't say a close friend, but they were always glad to see each other. Florence is shyer, more reserved, more of an innocent than Dyana was: Dyana was more "modern" and independent in her outlook and behaviour. We might have been rather shocked if she hadn't been such a warm person, so full of life. In addition to that, she was very pretty and had a wonderful sense of humour. Altogether a remarkable young woman, with outstanding qualities. She was longing for Denis to marry her, and I'm sure he'd have given way eventually.'

'But from what I hear he was rigidly opposed to it.'

'Yes, provisionally, and for perfectly sound reasons.'

'How do you think Wotan viewed the situation?'

'In my opinion – but you'll keep this to yourself! – he didn't think much of Dyana or his son, either. Admittedly, he regarded them as members of his household and his family; but he found Denis's political views and Dyana's general behaviour extremely irritating. I imagine he'd have preferred to have someone else as his daughter-in-law.'

'Someone like your daughter?' Holz suggested and received a black look from Dullac.

Wetzel gave an embarrassed titter. 'Well, since you ask . . . the idea had occurred to Florence . . . and to me. I'd have been pleased to see my family linked with the Grüns and our two businesses run in partnership: they're more or less complementary. I've cherished the dream of an association for a long time now: I even came near to buying up Wotan's business once.'

Dullac pricked up his ears. 'Really? When was that?'

'It must have been about a year ago. Wotan told me that he was in a tight corner financially, and we drew up a scheme: I was to buy the shop and workroom, but Wotan was to remain owner of the actual walls, as of the rest of the house, of course, and I was to retain him as bookbinder and manager, which meant that there wouldn't have been much change in his way of life. Naturally, he didn't much relish the idea, and I didn't press him to implement it. Then he suddenly sold some very fine folio volumes, which had almost certainly come from the Estienne brothers' workroom, for a large sum, and this put him back on his feet again. I was delighted for his sake, in spite of my own disappointment.'

'He must value your friendship.'

'I hope so. I value his. He's certainly got his faults: he's very self-centred, very dictatorial; but his faults are compensated for by his great generosity and a most attractive personality.'

'What do you make of his skirmish with Pastor Michelon?'

'Oh, so you've heard about that?' Wetzel said, surprised. 'Yes, it's quite true there was – what shall I call it? – a rift in our discussion group a few months ago.'

'What exactly did happen?'

'Well, some of us got rather tired of Wotan making all the decisions without consulting anyone. It all came to a head one evening when we were leaving. Everyone was saying "See you next Thursday" and Wotan took it into his head to add jokingly "Same time, same place" without realizing that he was presenting his opponents with an opening. Alice de Potztausend promptly demanded "Why the same place? Why don't we change our surroundings? I've got a large library where we'd all be very comfortable." You can imagine the look on Wotan's face as he listened to a proposal that must have struck him as close to high treason. But he got an even worse shock when the Pastor and young Schwarz supported the poetess's suggestion. It suddenly dawned on him that talk had been going on behind his back.'

'How did he answer them?'

'Majestically, of course. "I've no wish to stop you entertaining your friends," he said stiffly to Madame de Potztausend. "I myself shall be entertaining mine next Thursday where we are now." After that we all left, rather embarrassed. During the week the Pastor's wife and Alice called on him to ask him to reconsider the proposal, but he wouldn't hear of it. On the following Thursday there were several regulars missing: some of them had rung up with invented excuses; others had not bothered to show him this courtesy – or hypocrisy, whichever you like to call it. The future of the discussion group seemed to be seriously threatened, but finally, after several weeks had passed without Wotan giving any signs of changing his attitude, the lost sheep returned to the fold – apart from the Michelons, who stuck to their guns.'

'What frame of mind had Wotan been in during this period?'

'He was very angry and very contemptuous. He didn't make any attempt to conciliate the rebels, but I'm sure he was delighted when they surrendered.'

'What did they have to say about it?'

'That it had been high time to teach Wotan a lesson and that the incident would have done him good. At least, that's what Dyana told my daughter.'

'Dyana? What had she to do with it? Surely she didn't attend the meetings?'

'No, I doubt if we saw her three times in four years! She got her information from the young painter.'

'Schwarz?'

'Yes, he was doing her portrait at the time. You may have seen it?'

'Yes, I have.'

'And a very good portrait it is, too. He's got real talent, Superintendent. I know what I'm talking about.'

'Do you remember which members took part in the rebellion?'

'Yes, I can tell you if you're interested: the poetess, the Michelons and young Schwarz. But they didn't all behave in the same way. For instance, the Michelons didn't allow any ill feeling to creep into the defence of their stand: I've remained on good terms with them, although I'm a Catholic. And, of course, being neighbours, it'd have been very awkward if there'd been a coolness between us. There were some people who took no part in the rebellion, but were affected by it to some degree. Andros's daughter was torn between her father's neutrality and the commitment of the young painter, whom she was making eyes at. And Claire, whose insubordinate tendencies drew her towards the cabal, felt as a Grün that she should support her father. The attitude of the two psychiatrists was the most complex of all. They had appeared to be unequivocally on the side of the dissidents and, at a meeting they had attended at Madame de Potztausend's, had not hesitated to brand the absent Wotan as a megalomaniac; yet, on the following Thursday, they were the only ones of their group to turn up again at Wotan's, where they were all over him.'

'Sincerity scarcely seems to be their strong point!'

'To tell you the truth, I dislike psychiatrists in general and those two most of all. I don't think they're right in the head.'

'People always say that about psychiatrists,' Dullac observed.

'And they're dead right! What drives a man or woman to adopt that profession if it isn't their personal proclivities?'

'There could be something in that,' Dullac admitted,

'but I have to steer clear of prejudices.'

'That does you credit, Superintendent,' Wetzel said solemnly. 'It's what I would have expected from a man of your reputation.'

Dullac thanked him with equal solemnity; then he and Holz left.

2

'Monsieur Dullac!' Alice Reine-Camyon de Potztausend exclaimed delightedly as she opened the front door of her large elegant house in the Rue Saint-Maurice to the two detectives. 'Come in! Come in! I was just about to go out but, for a friend like you, I'll put it off.'

To her visitors, the last of the Potztausends appeared to be dressed for battle; greenish-grey tweeds, butter-coloured gauntlets with shoes to match, and a musketeer's hat adorned with an emerald-green feather. She was a tall, solidly built woman with broad shoulders, a square determined chin, and alert, expressive eyes. She admitted to being fifty, was a good ten years older and, as the blondeness of her hair owed little to nature, might have been taken for Wotan Grün's first cousin. Following in her wake, the detectives crossed a tiled floor, climbed a broad curving staircase and entered the library that Wetzel had mentioned. The windows looked out on a formal, well-kept garden. Shelves running round the walls displayed a large number of valuable, beautifully bound books, some of them the product of the Grün workroom. In the centre of the room low tables and enormous leather armchairs, old and shabby but extremely comfortable, were an invitation to read or merely relax. At a sign from their hostess the two men sat down.

'No, not there!' Alice boomed out; then, when Holz was too much taken aback to move, explained, 'You've got your back to the light: I can't see your features. I've always looked men straight in the face; surely you don't expect me to change my habits at my age?'

Holz sheepishly moved to another chair and Madame de Potztausend sat down in the one he had vacated.

'I know, I know . . . Now it's you who can't see me. Well, you'll just have to grin and bear it. When we reach the final grilling and you've got me locked up in one of those sinister offices of yours at Police Headquarters, you'll be in a position to shine all the spotlights you want into my eyes.'

'We haven't quite reached that stage yet,' Dullac told her, smiling.

'That's just what I was pointing out,' she retorted and went on without a pause, 'So they bumped her off, did they? The poor child! So young! So pretty! And so charming! She adored my poems. Have you read *The Flowers in my Garden?*'

Dullac answered tactfully and shamelessly that he had not yet had that pleasure but that one of his colleagues had spoken very highly of it. It earned him a carnivorous smile from the authoress.

'I had no idea that police officers took such interest in artistic matters,' she said delightedly. 'Remind me later to give you an autographed copy. I had it published at my own expense and I still have several hundred copies in the attic. Can you imagine that pretentious idiot Grün refused to do the binding when I asked him to, just because I suggested he might make me a special price in view of our friendship? The poor child!' she continued without any apparent relevance. 'To go like that, cut off in the flower of her youth! Still, if she had lived she would probably have become Madame Grün. Which fate strikes you as the more appalling?'

'Well, as Molière said, it's better to be married than dead,' Dullac answered.

'No doubt, no doubt! Except when the fiancé's name is Grün. When Wotan's first wife died I was aware that I had only to say the word to slip into the unfortunate woman's bed while it was still warm. But I didn't utter that word! Wotan was terribly upset, but he's a proud man and never made any allusion to it. It was only our eyes that spoke. Shortly afterwards, he met that little Edwige girl. Too young. Much too young! It simply goes to prove that every man, even an artist like Wotan, allows himself to be carried away by his sensuality and appetite for enjoyment.' She addressed Holz, 'I was certainly right to make you move, young man. You've got a most romantic face. What's your name?'

'Inspector Holz, Madame la Comtesse,' Holz told her, stressing the 'Inspector', but it did not appear to register.

'Delightful! Quite delightful! There's one thing, though: I'm not a Countess. I'm a Baroness. Not that it matters in the least,' she added, waving aside Holz's apologies before he had time to utter them.

At this juncture, there was the sound of furious scratching on one of the library's doors.

'Mah-jong! My treasure! My little chinkie! Guess who's here!' the poetess exclaimed, walking to the door and holding it wide open.

On the threshold was a tiny pekinese, which she picked up and carried over to the two men. 'Your great friend, Superintendent Dullac! You remember him, don't you? He's the one who took so much trouble to find you when you were lost. Come along, Superintendent, say how-do-you-do to your great friend.'

She firmly planted the dog on the Superintendent's knees. Concealing his feelings, Dullac began gently scratching the animal's ears.

'He recognizes you!' the poetess declared, completely forgetting that the Superintendent and the dog had never previously set eyes on each other.

'It just shows what intelligence, memory and fidelity these tiny beasts possess,' Dullac said solemnly.

Though the word 'beasts' made her wince, Madame de Potztausend was only too happy to endorse the Superintendent's observation and came up with a profound one of her own. 'A lot of men are vastly inferior to certain animals. That's what I wanted to bring out in my famous sonnet, which I'm sure you know, Superintendent; the one that begins:

"*Come, give me your paw, and catch a chockie-wockie!*" '

With apparent sincerity Dullac assured her that the line was frequently quoted, not only in Strasbourg but throughout the Bas-Rhin.

'And in Paris, too,' she said sharply. 'I gave several copies of my book to a bookseller friend of mine in the Latin Quarter and one still comes across them today among the second-hand booksellers on the Left Bank.'

Dullac and Holz managed to assume appropriate expressions of admiration, but by now the strain was beginning to tell, and Dullac decided to bring her back to the point.

'Talking of Dyana Pasquier . . . '

'I didn't kill her!' the poetess cut in, emphasizing her denial with such a lofty gesture that her huge hat slid down over one ear. Irritated by the mishap, she snatched the hat off and deposited it on a nearby chair.

'No one questions your innocence,' Dullac said hurriedly, 'but every statement can prove helpful, particularly if it comes from someone gifted with observation and intuition.'

For a moment he was afraid that he might have laid on the flattery too thick, but he was quickly reassured. There was no shadow of suspicion in the devastating smile he received in response.

'Well, you've certainly come to the right person! There's not much I don't know about the Grüns. If I were to tell you everything . . . but I won't.'

Dullac pointed out that this was the subject that interested him the most.

'Vulgar tittle-tattle?' the poetess exclaimed in the same tone of utter disgust and outraged majesty that Marie-Antoinette might have employed when saying, 'Let them eat cake!'

Summoning his last reserves of patience, Dullac insisted, 'This is a case where the end excuses any distastefulness in the means. Justice pursuing Crime must be an allegory that appeals to you.' He regretted this last sentence as soon as he had uttered it, fearing that this might be a theme on which the Baroness had composed another of her sonnets; but his alarm was not justified. Apparently she found her inspiration in dogs, cats and flowers rather than in the more notable allegories.

'Very well,' she said finally with a show of reluctance, 'if in a way it's a crusade, we'll go ahead and drive vice out of Strasbourg. You can count on me, my boy,' she added more prosaically, striking Dullac on the knee with such force that he could not repress a groan. 'I knew it would end in disaster. It was obvious. She was a charming girl, but she came from a completely different background. Why, she wasn't even Alsatian! She was a southerner. That's almost the same as a foreigner. Actually, no one quite knew where she came from. It may have been the north. Anyway, she didn't come from around here. If I'd been Wotan, I'd have put a stop to their . . . irregular relationship. It was enough to shock even the most tolerant-minded, of whom I flatter myself I'm one. What's more, in my opinion Denis wasn't so foolish as he appeared: he didn't want to marry her. She, naturally, did everything she could to make him and who can blame her? She was merely looking after her own interests. But who knows to what lengths a man will go when he's in love? . . . I do,' she added after a moment's reflection, 'I do only too well, but that's another story . . . Anyway, Denis finally gave in, and the Grüns' name was about to be disgraced. Wotan realized that it was too late for him to try to assert his paternal authority, so he took matters into his own hands, and he was quite right to do so. I fully approve. It's better to have blood on one's hands than a blot on one's name, don't you agree?'

Out of his depth, Dullac observed, 'If I follow you, you're accusing Wotan Grün of the murder?'

'Of the act of justice, Superintendent! Surely I don't need to remind you that the head of a family has the right of life and death over the lost sheep in his flock? And anyway,' she added illogically, 'Wotan has no respect whatever for human life except, of course, his own.'

'Forgive me,' Dullac said politely, but there was a sharper note in his voice, 'but I seem to have heard that you had a disagreement with Wotan Grün some months ago?'

In spite of the strategic position she was occupying, the two men could still catch the shade of annoyance that crossed the old woman's face.

'Oh, you knew that?' she snapped, then went on more calmly, 'Well, yes, it's quite true. Grün was extremely discourteous to me and some of my friends. He's much too self-important! One longs to tell him "Do stop regarding yourself as God's gift to mankind!" Consequently, the Pastor and I felt fully justified in proposing that the site of our meetings should alternate between the various members' houses. Wotan showed himself in his true colours by flatly refusing, and proved that the real object of our meetings wasn't, as he claimed, to become better acquainted with beauty in all its forms, but merely to satisfy his own arrogance. It was a great disappointment to me,' she added, heaving a sigh of disillusion, 'but I'm used to that. My life has been a long series of trials and misfortunes. One day I'll tell you about them.'

As much to avoid this alarming prospect as from a sense

of duty, Dullac switched the conversation to the events on the evening of the crime in so far as the poetess knew them. Unfortunately, this produced no new item of information, merely confirmed what he knew already: the quarrel between Claire and her father, the subjects discussed at the meeting, Wotan's departure for the Weberstub at ten-thirty, accompanied by herself, Wilfrid-Hamlet Boersen and the two Gruaus, and the arrival there shortly after of Edwige and then Claire. She also confirmed that none of these various people left the table until two-thirty in the morning, when the closure of the Weberstub compelled the party to break up.

Finally, bearing with them a collection of her poems, inscribed 'To the great friend of my faithful four-legged companion', Dullac and Holz left her, immensely relieved to find themselves back again in the crisp fresh air.

3

'Delighted to meet you, Superintendent,' the Pastor said warmly as he entered the small drawing-room, where Dullac and Holz were already sitting with his wife.

The Michelons' house, next to the church, stood on the river bank by the Pont Saint-Martin. The Grüns' impressive house was only a short distance away, while, nearer still, only separated from the church by the length of the bridge, was the Weberstub.

Dullac took an immediate liking to the Pastor. The two men had not met before and the Superintendent, he scarcely knew why, had expected an elderly man to come in. Robert Michelon was far from that, being forty-five at the most: he was thin, well-tailored, with thick iron-grey hair, and a moustache trimmed in the latest style, so that he had more the appearance of a socialite than a minister of the gospel. His sparkling almond eyes seemed to be screwed up in a perpetual smile that was frequently accompanied by a loud laugh which displayed an excellent set of teeth.

Taking after her husband, Madame Michelon in no way conformed to the conventional idea of a clergyman's wife. In her early forties, discreetly but skilfully made-up, with a hair-style that suited her admirably, carefully manicured nails, and a simple dress in bright colours that obviously came from an expensive shop, she, too, could have been a member of the fashionable middle-class Strasbourg set.

'These gentlemen have come to see us about the little Pasquier girl,' she informed her husband as he sat down facing the visitors.

'What a tragedy! There's a rumour going round that she was murdered?'

Dullac remarked that, for once, rumour wasn't lying.

'It's really most distressing. A terrible blow for young Denis. But I can't see in what way my wife and I can be of help to you.'

'I gather you haven't seen much of the Grüns lately,' Dullac observed, assuming his guileless expression.

The Pastor laughed good-humouredly. 'Now, Superintendent, you don't have to play the innocent to get the truth out of me. It's obvious that the murder must have set tongues clacking, so you'll have been told twenty times what caused our breach with the Grüns.'

Amused by his candour, Dullac laughed, too. 'I admit it. But the versions varied from one person to the next.'

'That can scarcely have surprised you! Surely you come across that in all your investigations? It's the same in everyday life. Everyone has his own version of the truth. For what it's worth, I'll give you mine: like all of us here below, Wotan has his share of good qualities and his share of faults. My wife and I admired him for his good qualities; we parted from him because of his faults. The idea of transferring our meetings from his workroom to other members' houses originated with Madame de Potztausend, our local poetess.'

'We've just come from her,' Dullac told him with a grimace that set the Pastor off into another burst of his infectious laughter.

'Then let me offer you a drink. You must need one!'

While Madame Michelon attended to it, her husband went on, 'I suspect that dear Alice's motives were not entirely blameless. To tell you the truth, there was a time when she had what's known as a "crush" on the fascinating Wotan. Without any chance of it being reciprocated, I need hardly say!' Once again the Pastor laughed. 'My friend Wotan prefers young, unsophisticated girls. Alice worked herself up into a jealous rage, which led her to sift through the various ways she could hurt Wotan for the one that would wound him the most. And to do her justice, she chose with great discernment.'

Surprised, Dullac asked, 'But if you knew that. why did you back her?'

'Because, though we disapproved of her motives, we were in agreement with her objective. And some other members joined us. So there was – if I dare call it that – a schism. As far as I was concerned, the amusing part of the whole affair was that, while I found myself in the dissidents' camp, my opposite number, Father Doppelleben, found himself in the conservatives' camp. The religious wars were starting up again.'

'What's your opinion of the Reverend Father?'

'Well, for a Catholic, he's not too bad!' The loud laughter rang out again.

'He's a very good man,' Madame Michelon put in kindly. 'He loves children.'

'He also loves consorting with the eminent,' the Pastor added rather less kindly. 'Nothing on earth would make him fall out with the Grüns. Things soon came to a head, and when I saw that one by one those who had spoken loudest and with the greatest bitterness were giving in to Wotan, I must confess I felt rather disgusted. So, by way of protest, my wife and I decided to resign from the discussion group.'

'How did Wotan take it?'

'Oh, like God the Father when he discovered that Adam and Eve had munched the apple. In his eyes, we hadn't left: he'd expelled us.'

'What sort of terms have you been on with the Grüns since the breach?'

It was Madame Michelon who answered. 'Oh, very polite. When we pass a member of the family in the street we always greet each other. But we aren't on visiting terms any more.'

'You haven't kept up with any of the other members of the group?'

'Yes, we've remained close friends with Florent Wetzel. As you know, he's our neighbour. It's his house you see over there.' The Pastor gestured towards the window.

'There's one thing that surprises me,' Dullac said as though it had suddenly occurred to him, though in fact it had been puzzling him for some time. 'The night the body was found, Wetzel didn't go to the Weberstub with the Grüns. As soon as the meeting broke up, he went back home with his daughter. Shortly before dawn, a witness spotted the body floating in the river between your windows and those in the Grüns' house.'

'Yes, it was Madame Dickbauch. She's one of my flock, and has described the shock it gave her at considerable length.'

'Well, now, she started shrieking at the top of her voice and a crowd soon gathered. When I arrived shortly afterwards at Gräber's bar, where everyone had gone to get warm, I found nearly all the residents in the district milling round her. In particular, Wetzel was there. But you . . . you weren't. Didn't you hear anything?'

'I certainly did! I'm a light sleeper, and those screams under my window at four o'clock in the morning could hardly have failed to wake me. Like everyone else, I got up and went over to the window. I saw a crowd of people but I couldn't make out what was going on. They were just too far away for me to recognize Madame Dickbauch. I thought it must be some drunks quarrelling and in view of the numbers already on the spot, I did not feel that there was any need for me to intervene. As for going out just to

MONDAY   105

have a look, I don't possess that kind of curiosity. What actually did happen?'

Dullac told him briefly. After reflecting on his account for a moment, the Pastor remarked, 'That business of the body disappearing, then turning up again is quite extraordinary. What can be the explanation? Have you a theory, Superintendent?'

'Yes, I have and I think it's the right one. But, as you'll understand . . . '

'Of course! Of course! If a clergyman doesn't know the demands of professional secrecy, who does?'

And the interview ended as it had begun, with a burst of laughter.

4

'What about young Schwarz?'

'He's been told to come to your office at ten o'clock tomorrow morning.'

Dullac gave a nod of approval. The two detectives were lunching at the Weberstub, and had chosen a table in a corner by the window, from which they could look out on the pleasant landscape of the river and the Pont Saint-Martin, but also – and this gave them less enjoyment – on the Grüns' house and the Dentelles cul-de-sac.

A pretty waitress brought them the *tourte vigneronne*, crusty and hot, and a bottle of Pinot Noir – 'an extravagance', Dullac pointed out, since his salary did not normally permit him to indulge in such luxuries; but it was an occasion when both men felt the need of it.

The head waiter, who had spotted them from a distance, and like all good head waiters could recognize policemen at first glance, hurried up.

'I hope everything's to your satisfaction ... er . . . Inspector?'

It was a direct question and Dullac amiably answered it. 'Nearly right. Superintendent, actually. Chief Superintendent Dullac, and this is Inspector Holz.'

'It's a great honour to have you here, gentlemen,' the waiter assured them, though, from his expression, it did not appear to be one he appreciated.

'You might be in a position to help us if you were on duty last Thursday evening.'

'I'm always on duty,' the waiter said sourly.

'Then perhaps you can remember whether the Grün family were here that evening?'

'Yes, I remember them being here.'

'Can you tell me when they arrived?'

'On the stroke of half-past ten, as usual. They came in separately – first Monsieur Wotan and Madame de Potztausend, the Boersen boy and the two psychiatrists. I don't care for them: they told me once that I had a complex.'

Dullac looked shocked. 'How did they get that idea?'

'I don't know. We always have a chat when they're here. I happened to say that this place meant a lot of work because, with our three floors, we run a bar, a discotheque and a restaurant. "Yes, yes," they said, "you've got a fine complex there." '

Dullac and Holz, to their credit, kept straight faces. 'I shouldn't worry,' Dullac told him kindly. 'Psychiatrists are like detectives: they're always wrapped up in their profession.'

'Ah, yes, that must be it,' the waiter said, relieved. 'Well, going back to Thursday, they can't have been here more than twenty minutes before Madame Edwige joined them. And five minutes after that, Mademoiselle Claire turned up.'

'And Denis?'

'Oh, Monsieur Denis scarcely ever comes to the Weberstub. It's not a place for him, he's far too serious-minded and proper. The one time he did come, he nearly made a scene: he called the clients "decadent swine". Yes, I'm sorry to say it, but those were his actual words, "decadent swine". In my opinion, he's a very correct, well-brought-up young man, quite unlike all the young people today who only dream of starting revolutions.'

Unseen by the waiter, the two detectives exchanged ironic glances.

'And did all these people – I mean, the Grüns and their friends – strike you as being just the same as usual?' Dullac asked.

'Yes, the same as always. Though Mademoiselle Claire did look a little worked up when she arrived.'

'Worked up?'

'Yes. Or you might say put out. At first I thought something must have happened to annoy her, but it didn't last long; she was soon talking and laughing in her normal way.'

'Tell me: did any one of them leave the table at any time?'

'I don't think so. There were a lot of people at their

table, people who weren't in their party, and they'd have had to squeeze past them to get out. It would have caused a stir and I'd have been certain to notice it.'

'What time did they leave?'

'Well, we close at two o'clock sharp and make everyone leave within the next ten minutes. But we make an exception with the Grüns: we always let their party go on chatting while we start clearing up. Usually they leave of their own accord at half-past two and that's what they did that evening.'

'If I follow you, they were the last people left in the room. So, if one of them had slipped out beforehand, you'd have noticed?'

'Yes. Quite definitely.'

'Thank you. I don't see anything else to ask you,' Dullac concluded; then, when the waiter had bowed himself away out of earshot, added disgustedly, 'Actually, I don't see anything at all. If one of that lot murdered Dyana Pasquier, I'll be willingly transferred to a desert island!'

5

The afternoon was cold but bright. The sun had been shining for five hours as though determined to dissociate itself from the gloom propagated by the recent tragedy.

'We'll separate here to save time,' Dullac said to his subordinate as they left the restaurant. 'I'll leave the two Androses and young Boersen to you. You'd better see Denis Grün's friend, Charles Feldmann, too. And while you're about it, ring up Jacques Schiller's friend in Colmar – the one he says he spent Thursday night with – and check the various statements and alibis we've been given with each one of them. I'll tackle Doppelleben, the two Gruaus and Dyana's closest friend, Martine.'

'Shall I report to you this evening?'

'No, that won't be necessary. You can have the evening off. Though now I come to think of it, the easiest way to get hold of Germain Andros would be to go to the evening performance at the Comédie du Rhin. Why not seize the opportunity to extend your theatrical education?' Ignoring Holz's grimace, Dullac added, 'Be at my office tomorrow morning when I'm questioning young Schwarz. After that, we'll see how far we've got . . . if anywhere. Have a pleasant evening! Enjoy yourself, and don't fall asleep: I'll expect you to give me an account of the play.'

And with this Parthian arrow, the Superintendent went on his way.

6

A fair-haired, blue-eyed boy of twelve or under opened the front door of Father Dominique Doppelleben's flat to Dullac.

'The Father won't be a minute,' he said, as he ushered him into a large sitting-room, furnished with an eye to comfort and sound craftsmanship.

And, bearing him out, the Father appeared almost immediately. Once again, Dullac was surprised: he had expected to see a short, stoutish man and found himself faced by a tall, thin one with a scholarly, ascetic face. But the face was smiling graciously, doing its best to welcome him warmly.

'Superintendent!' the priest acknowledged him formally in a soft, almost feminine voice and waved him with long, tapering fingers to a Chippendale chair – no doubt worth a fortune. 'Your lesson's over now, Marc,' he said, turning to the boy, 'so you can run along home. Give my regards to your mother.'

He waited for the boy to leave the room before commenting, 'That's my life, Superintendent; entirely devoted to the instruction of souls. In the afternoon, here at home, I teach the young ones; in the morning, at the university, I teach theology to their elders. I've no other ambition than to win souls over to God's cause in this way, and, in a world where the moral virtues tend more and more to disappear, I consider one must set about it as early as possible when those souls have not yet been corrupted by society, so as to give full effect to the sacred utterance, "Suffer little children to come unto me." But I am trespassing on your time, and I regret it, because your mission here below goes hand in hand with mine: I preach virtue, you quell vice.'

'That's a very idyllic vision of a policeman's job, Father, but I'm grateful for the good opinion you have of it. But to come to the purpose of my visit . . . I imagine you've guessed it?'

'I've read the newspapers and it appears that you're faced with a case of murder. Poor child! I immediately penned a few words of friendship to the Grüns – I say "of friendship" and not "of condolence" because, after all, Dyana was not really related to them. Don't think I'm sectarian or retrograde, I keep up with the times; but, all the same, this liaison had been going on for four years, and, for the last three, she had been living under the family roof. On many occasions I told my friend Wotan how desirable it seemed to me for the two of them to get married and so regularize their dubious relationship; but he merely laughed. "Denis is young," he used to say. "Let him wait a little before putting a rope round his neck!" '

'That sounds typically Wotan Grün!'

'And today, look what's happened! The child has died in sin. Have you any idea who was responsible?'

Dullac laughed. 'One of my reasons for coming here was to ask you the same question.'

'Forgive me, but how could I possibly know? That evening I left the Grüns' house, as I do every Thursday, at half-past ten, and came straight back here.'

'Quite! But I hoped you might be able to tell me something that would give me a lead . . . a remark you overheard, a look you weren't meant to see . . . I realize I'm on delicate ground, but . . . '

'No, no, I quite understand. You're seeking for a motive and you're seeking for it among the members of the family and those of the discussion group. Am I right?'

'Unless the murder was a fortuitous one, committed, for example, by a burglar caught on the job, one has to look for the murderer among the victim's relations and friends.'

'Yes, that seems reasonable. Unfortunately, the mem-

bers of the discussion group had no apparent contact with
Dyana, apart from young Schwarz, who was a friend of
hers and painted her portrait. She took no interest in our
meetings: I suspect she was afraid of being bored. As far as
the Grün family's concerned, Wotan clearly disliked her,
but that scarcely means that he'd be prepared to murder
her! Claire and Jacques Schiller, on the other hand,
seemed very fond of her.'

The Father lapsed into silence. Dullac remained silent,
too, waiting for one more name, one that the priest had not
yet mentioned. When this was not forthcoming and the
silence dragged on, he decided to take the plunge.

'And . . . Edwige?'

Was it just his imagination or had Father Doppelleben
repressed a look of annoyance before replying, 'Edwige?'

'Yes, Edwige. What sort of terms was she on with
Dyana?'

'They were polite,' the priest said after another pause.

'Yes, I understand that. But were they warm?'

Father Doppelleben seemed to see a possible line of
escape. 'Haven't you already had an answer to that from
other people?'

'Yes, but their opinions have differed. According to
some, their relationship was cordial . . . '

'That's what I said: polite.'

'According to others, Edwige envied Dyana.'

The priest gave a sigh of relief. 'I'm glad you heard that.
I shan't have the feeling that I'm betraying a confidence.'

'A confidence?'

'Edwige Grün confided in me.'

'She spoke to you about envying Dyana?'

'Yes . . . But don't get the idea that she disliked her. Quite the contrary! Edwige was very much attracted to Dyana by her complete freedom of speech and behaviour. Dyana had achieved what she herself lacked: independence.'

'Did she regret her marriage to Wotan, then?'

'It's not as simple as that. To begin with, Edwige comes from a family of very modest means. Her education involved her parents in considerable sacrifice.'

'It was the same for mine,' Dullac observed feelingly.

'Her marriage to Grün meant the end of poverty and the beginning of a life of ease.'

'So she married him for money?'

'No! No! I told you it's not so simple. *Edwige loves Wotan.* She *genuinely* loves him.'

'Did she tell you so?'

'She did, and it's quite apparent to anyone who sees them together. It's common knowledge that women find Wotan attractive. His physique, his authority, his fortune, and you can add his age, were so many additional trump cards in captivating Edwige; for to her he represented a prop and a bulwark; in short, she felt safe. And for some time everything went like clockwork: Edwige dozed the days away, tranquil and happy.'

'And then . . . ?'

'A young man appeared.'

'Ah!'

'Yes, a young man. Nothing more but nothing less.'

'Who was he?'

'Oh, some boy from Colmar, a student.'

'How did she come to meet him?'

'He was a friend of Jacques Schiller's.'

'What was his name?'

'I've forgotten,' the priest said.

'When did this happen?'

'A year ago. Personally, I believe that Helen genuinely loved Menelaus. But Paris was so young and handsome!'

'Did she become his mistress?'

'No. Once again, it couldn't work out as simply as that. She . . . How shall I put it? . . . *She came out of her trance.* She rediscovered a young, very young girl. But this young girl was Wotan Grün's wife. So, curtain!'

'Which explains why she resented Dyana?'

'Yes, and Denis too, for continually putting off their wedding. If the young couple had got married she'd immediately have become friends with Dyana, because then there would no longer have been anything to come between them. Dyana would have become *a Grün*, too.'

Dullac mentally paid tribute to Claire's perspicacity: what he had just heard confirmed all her theories.

'Did Wotan know?'

'Now that would have produced a nice scandal! No, Edwige only confided in two people.'

'You.'

'Yes.'

'And?'

'Dyana.'

'Dyana!'

'Yes, and if you think about it, it's not so surprising. A young man had found Edwige attractive, and she'd been put in a flutter by him. Nothing could give her more plea-sure than to prove to Dyana that she wasn't tucked away on a shelf any more than Dyana was.'

'So Dyana shared her secret. Do you suppose she kept it to herself?'

'There's every reason to think so, for nothing ever leaked out. Neither Wotan nor Denis ever gave an inkling of suspecting or knowing anything.'

'When all's said and done,' Dullac remarked, 'Edwige did nothing wrong. It was just a passing fancy.'

He had intended it to be a question, but the priest looked him straight in the eye without answering, and he did not persist. He got up, murmured a few words of thanks and left. As he started down the staircase he passed a brown-haired, dark-eyed boy of twelve or less coming up and smiling at the priest, who was still standing on the landing. And he heard the priest greet him with, 'Good afternoon, Luc. How is your dear mother?'

7

The Gruaus, Gilbert and Janine, had a ground-floor flat in the Avenue de la Marseillaise, a short distance from the Comédie du Rhin. By a lucky chance Dullac found them both in. In a determinedly ultra-modern sitting-room, slightly reminiscent of a waiting-room in a clinic, all bare walls and parallel lines, from which every curve, obtuse and acute angle had been banished, they sat him in a chair constructed of steel tubes and nylon, which discharged into his hands the static electricity that he seemed to have accumulated in a distressingly high-powered form. After the first shock he took care to avoid touching the seat with his bare hands, and sat bolt upright on the edge of it with his legs close together. When the ash from his cigarette threatened to fall on the bare floor his hostess hurried over with a cubic ashtray, which she then meticulously replaced on a glass table, taking care to see that the edges of the cube were parallel with those of the table, and five centimetres away from them. Stunned, Dullac congratulated her on her tidiness.

'It's essential,' she answered with a shade of reproof in her voice. 'Tidiness in material things makes for a tidy mind. Isn't that so, Gilbert?'

'Yes, dear,' her husband agreed with a grimace. At first, Dullac thought it was directed at him but, when it recurred, he decided it was just a nervous tic, and felt better.

Taking a good look at his host and hostess, he found them young. Not much over twenty-five. Both of them had fair hair and equally solemn faces, but with a slight difference: in the woman's case the solemnity was an intentional seriousness; in the man's case, it clothed an expression of dejection. During the quarter of an hour that his visit lasted, Dullac did not see either of them smile even once.

'I've come to see you in connection with Dyana Pasquier's death,' he started off, but before he could get any further the woman cut in.

'It was bound to happen.'

'That I came to see you?'

'That, too, I suppose. But I was referring to the suicide.'

'It wasn't suicide,' Dullac tried to explain, but was cut short again.

'Oh, come, now! The girl couldn't endure life any longer, couldn't endure herself any longer. We warned Wotan, didn't we, Gilbert?'

'Yes, dear,' Gilbert answered, leaning forward.

'Do sit up straight, Gilbert!'

Gilbert sat up straight.

'Dyana Pasquier was mentally unstable,' Janine went on. 'Unstable and a nymphomaniac. Incurable, I'm afraid, as she regarded herself as perfectly healthy.'

'Actually, she was described to me as a very healthy young woman,' Dullac observed.

'Nonsense! She was a deeply troubled person, who was hoping to find in Denis the solid family nucleus and heavy father she so sadly lacked.'

'Yet she appears to have been extremely cheerful and charming, full of humour, self-confident, loving life and the people around her; glad to be alive, in fact.'

'Exactly! All that isn't normal. Her taste for pleasure and zest for life are the certain symptoms of neurosis. Life, Superintendent, consists of restraint and duty. What we are is detestable, so we must restrain and reform ourselves. Isn't that so, Gilbert?'

'Yes, dear,' Gilbert replied with another grimace.

Dullac persisted. 'But didn't she do her duty and even more than her duty in working as she did?'

'Now there you've hit on an interesting point. The pleasure she took in working and remaining independent clearly concealed an acute feeling of frustration. Or, alternatively, an inferiority complex induced by Denis's intellectualism, which led her to adopt this method to humiliate and enslave him. It's hardly the way to promote a harmonious relationship. You agree, don't you, Gilbert?'

Dullac nearly found himself replying, 'Yes, dear,' before Gilbert actually did so.

'You've certainly given me something to think about,' he told Janine. 'If I followed your train of thought correctly, the people who appear to be the least troubled are, in fact, the most afflicted?'

'Precisely!' Janine agreed. 'What's more, it's necessary.'

'For whom?'

'For us! It isn't a question of "it's necessary to have psychiatrists because there are sufferers from neuroses", but of "it's necessary to have sufferers from neuroses for there to be psychiatrists". '

'That's very enlightening,' Dullac said gravely.

'Yes, dear,' Gilbert put in, determined not to be left out.

'In other words,' Janine went on, 'the troubled and unstable constitute our bread and butter. Imagine a world of happy, relaxed people: there'd be nothing for us to do but recycle ourselves!'

And perhaps, too, there'd be fewer crimes of violence, Dullac thought, recalling with a pang Dyana's lifeless body and swollen face. But he kept the thought to himself, and asked his hostess for her opinion of Wotan Grün.

'A megalomaniac!' she declared without a moment's hesitation. 'Thirst for power. Tyrannical authoritarianism. And a very good friend,' she added. 'Isn't that so, Gilbert?'

'Absolutely, my dear,' Gilbert answered.

Well, well, a variation at last! Dullac reflected, then asked, 'What was that story I heard about a dispute and a schism rocking your discussion group?'

'It was megalomania precisely that was at the root of it. Old Potztausend – she's a schizophrenic, by the way – wanted us to meet at her house. She did it to get at Wotan, needless to say. All the same, we supported her, my husband and I, out of friendship for Wotan Grün.'

A look of perplexity crossed Dullac's face as he said, 'Forgive me, but I didn't quite get that. It was out of friendship for Wotan Grün that you sided against him?'

'Therapeutic. Shock treatment. Deprive him of his discussion group so as to make him come to terms with his vanity.'

'Did you have any success?'

'No. The others deserted us: they went back to Wotan,' she said, forgetting that she and her husband had not even left him. 'So, inevitably, it produced the opposite effect: he saw it as an additional proof of his omnipotence.'

'Yes, naturally,' Dullac said. 'I'm most grateful for all the valuable information you've given me.'

'I only did my duty.'

'There's just one final question I'd like to ask: how did you spend the evening of the crime?'

'Why?' Gilbert Gruau demanded abruptly, jumping up from his chair. 'Are we suspects?'

'Gilbert! Where's your self-control?' his wife snapped, getting up, too.

'Forgive me, my dear.' Gilbert sat down again.

'May I ask you – but more calmly – the same question as my husband?' Janine said, apparently deeply offended.

As she remained standing, Dullac felt obliged to rise cautiously from his own chair.

'There's no question of that,' he assured her. 'It's merely to enable me to check up on other people's alibis and timetables.'

'Very well, but let's cut it short. Eight-thirty: arrived at the meeting; ten-thirty: left for the Weberstub; half-past two in the morning: left the Weberstub and came back here. Does that satisfy you?'

'Yes, admirably. But please tell me this: did you, either at the meeting or the Weberstub, notice whether one of your friends left or was away for a short time?'

'As far as the Weberstub is concerned, the answer is no. Neither the three Grüns nor Boersen nor Alice, any more than my husband and I, left the table for a second. As for the meeting, there was of course Claire's very noticeable exit, but I imagine you've already heard about that from other people?'

Dullac admitted that this was the case as Janine moved disdainfully over to the door and held it open.

As he walked away, Dullac passed by the half-open sitting-room window, which permitted him to hear Janine addressing her husband in peremptory tones: 'Gilbert! Your tablets!'

'Yes, dear,' came the not wholly unexpected reply.

8

'Mademoiselle Martine Blitz?'

'Yes, that's me.'

The light-brown hair framed an impudent face that Dullac found rather prepossessing. And her studio flat was decorated and furnished with taste. Just the sort of girl to be a friend of Dyana Pasquier.

She suffered his scrutiny without embarrassment. 'Have you come about Dyana?'

A purely formal question: what other reason could he have had for coming? He nodded and waited stoically for her to go on. But she didn't.

'Well . . . ?' he asked, surprised.

'Well, what?'

'I was waiting for something like "It's dreadful!" or "What a tragedy!" That's all I've been hearing for the last three days.'

'I see,' she said. 'Would you like some coffee?'

'Bless you!'

Martine went into her lilliputian kitchen. He could watch her actions through the open door and it occurred to him that certain girls were decidedly well worth knowing: Martine, Dyana, Claire . . . This last name caused him a twinge in the neighbourhood of his stomach.

It's in one's heart, he reflected, that the twinge is popularly supposed to come. But that isn't true. It's one's stomach that is wrung. Poetry! Poetry! What inexactitudes are committed in thy name! But stomach or heart, the point is, do I know where I'm heading? Can I, whose profession it is to unravel enigmas, unravel that of my own life? You're thirty-five, my boy! You're losing your hair and putting on weight. If you ever intend to get married, perhaps now's the time to start thinking of it.

Martine's coffee drove his gloomy reflections away. It turned out to be strong enough to awaken the dead.

'Excellent!' he managed to blurt out.

Martine lit a cigarette and asked, 'What can I tell you that will help you?'

And Dullac thought, 'Now here's one who feels genuine sorrow; the sorrow that leaves nothing but a vast emptiness.'

'Where were you on the night of the crime?' he heard himself asking, almost automatically by now.

'At the Lorelei till half-past eleven. The other girls and the manager will confirm it. Then I came home, cooked myself some fried eggs and slept like a log till morning. At twelve o'clock Jacques came round to break the news to me.'

'Jacques Schiller?'

'Yes.'

'What were you doing between midnight and two o'clock?'

'I told you: I was here. Was that . . . Was that when it happened?'

'Yes.'

'Then I haven't an alibi.'

'Does it bother you?'

'No.'

'Why?'

'What earthly reason could I have had to . . . to do a thing like that? I've lost my closest friend.'

'I'd like to take your word for it.'

'But you aren't allowed to?'

'I have to check everything.'

'Yes, of course.'

'Her family, you know, believed she was here with you that night.'

'She often did stay here very late but she never slept here. I couldn't put her up comfortably, and anyway, she wouldn't have wanted to do that to Denis.'

'Did you dislike him?'

'No, I didn't. Why should I?'

'He didn't make her very happy.'

'She could have left him. As a matter of fact, she often spoke of it.'

'But she stayed?'

'Exactly!'

'Why did she stay?'

'Because she loved him, of course.'

'You're quite certain about that?'

'Absolutely!'

'So there was never any serious question of them separating?'

'Yes, once. But it was Denis who wanted to leave.'

'Really! When did that happen?'

'At the beginning of their affair. They were still living in his student's room. Things were very tough for them. Dyana had to pay for everything. Denis hadn't got his grant yet and they didn't want to take anything from Wotan. One day they had a row, and when Dyana got back from work Denis had gone, leaving a letter for her breaking things off. She rushed round at once to the Grüns', where she knew she'd find him, and it all ended in tears, hugs and a reconciliation. Dyana often spoke about it afterwards, and the happiness it had finally led to. She always kept Denis's letter in her bag and, whenever they looked like having a violent quarrel, she only had to show it to him to calm him down.'

'The talisman doesn't seem to have done its stuff recently.'

'No, relations between them became strained again.'

'Why? Because she wanted him to marry her?'

'Oh, she talked about it at the beginning, but she wasn't really all that keen on it. In the end, I believe she'd given up the idea altogether.'

'Did she tell you so?'

'No, she didn't, actually. She didn't tell me everything, you know.'

Dullac's eyebrows rose. 'Oh? I'd have imagined she would.'

'Then you'd have been wrong. Dyana was very proud. She didn't like to talk about her troubles, even to me. She always said, "Friends aren't there to be bored with one's problems." And when things were going badly she didn't come round here so often.' After a pause, she added, 'During these last few weeks she scarcely came at all.'

'That's interesting. It suggests she had a lot of worries.'

'Perhaps. Though she seemed more excited than worried. Once she said to me, "One of these days I'll tell you something." '

'She didn't say what about?'

'No. And I never used to ask any questions.'

'But you had some ideas of your own, surely?'

'Well, I thought – it's probably idiotic – that she'd found something out . . . a secret of some kind.'

'A family secret? Something about the Grüns?'

'Possibly. Or a secret about the fabrication of gold.'

'*About what?*' Dullac was thunderstruck. It was the last answer he had expected. He repeated, 'About the fabrication of gold?'

'Yes. Didn't you know that Wotan was investigating it?'

'No, I certainly didn't! I knew he was interested in alchemy, but I thought that meant in alchemy as a historical curiosity, not as a practical possibility; still less as one he might achieve himself.'

'It seems he found some things in an old book; things about the Philosopher's Stone and the whole caboodle.'

'Was it Dyana who told you that?'

'She said something about it, and so did Claire.'

'But it's impossible!' Dullac said, dazed. 'No one's ever transmuted lead, at least not in a way that was profitable. I can't make head or tail of it! And you say Claire mentioned it to you, too?'

'Yes, once; quite recently.'

'Are you very friendly with her?'

'Pretty friendly, yes. She often used to come and see me with Dyana. Jacques did, too.'

'And Edwige?'

'Edwige?'

'Yes. Did she come here, too?'

'Once. With Jacques.'

'How did she get on with you all?'

'She was very nice.'

'That's all?'

'That's all. Jacques was quite taken with her, but the three of us girls . . . '

'Were afraid of her?'

'Afraid of Wotan because of her. She's his wife and we didn't want him interfering in our fun.'

'What sort of fun?'

'Oh, it was perfectly harmless: we used to have a few drinks together, get up surprise parties, play practical jokes. We went over to Fribourg once to play lotto. If Edwige had known about it she might have told Wotan, and he'd have kicked up a fuss with Claire and Dyana.'

'Poor Edwige! And actually she's the same age as you are.'

'On her birth certificate, yes. But mentally she's Wotan's wife.'

'Poor Edwige!' Dullac repeated.

'It was her choice,' Martine said, concluding the interview.

9

It was ten o'clock in the evening of that same Monday. Dullac was at home alone, having dinner in front of his television. His steak was tough: he had not taken enough trouble in cooking it. But he was not hungry, anyway. Nor sleepy. He was obsessed by the case. The case . . . and a face. He could not make up his mind whether to go out again or not. The moonlight was inviting, but the biting cold was not. If only he was not so lonely . . .

Suddenly, the telephone rang. A presentiment made him hurry across the room to answer it.

'Is that Superintendent Dullac?'

He recognized the voice at once. 'Claire, my dear, what's wrong?'

The 'my dear' had slipped out involuntarily: he had never imagined that the strong-minded and unshakable young woman could be transformed into this panic-stricken, horrified being.

At the other end of the line, there was something close to a sob. 'Come! Come quickly! Someone's tried to kill my father!'

10

Once again the same distress, once again the nightmare. In his spacious drawing-room Wotan was lying on the sofa, being tended to and soothed by Edwige's diligent hands, and those of the family doctor. The bullet, fortunately, had only grazed his shoulder, and he had sustained no serious injury, but he had lost a lot of blood. Within a few minutes of his arrival Dullac had rung up his headquarters, and the police were now engaged in questioning the few pedestrians in the neighbourhood, and searching for the bullet in the hope that it might be somewhere about, and had not fallen into the river.

Denis was sitting in a state of shock by one of the windows, pale, drawn, and looking ten years older than when he had been questioned by Dullac on the previous Saturday.

'When will it stop?' he was muttering hysterically. 'There must be a curse on us!'

Claire was on her feet, clenching and unclenching her

fists. She seemed to have recovered some of her self-assurance, but Dullac would always remember her breathless voice on the telephone, and her expression of relief and gratitude when she had opened the door to him a little later.

Wetzel was there, too: he had assisted Denis in supporting Wotan back to the house.

Claire put Dullac in possession of the facts in a series of short sentences. Since Dyana's death, Wotan and Edwige had scarcely left the house. But this evening Wotan had suggested to her that they go round to the Weberstub to see a few of their friends and perhaps take their minds off the tragedy for an hour or two. Edwige had welcomed the suggestion: she felt a need to do something to ease the strain. Claire and Denis had stayed behind on their own, watching television. It must have been about half-past nine, shortly after the two Grüns had left, that there was the sound of an explosion in Petite France. Less than five minutes later Wetzel came rushing round and rang the front-door bell. When Claire and Denis answered it he told them that Wotan had just been shot on the Pont Saint-Martin and he needed their help to bring him back to the house. The three of them ran to the bridge, where Edwige, Florence Wetzel and a few onlookers were standing round Wotan, who was lying in a pool of blood, half-propped up against the foot of a street-lamp. Wetzel then proved himself to be a true friend by taking charge: he got rid of the spectators, sent Claire and Edwige ahead to prepare dressings and telephone the doctor and the Superintendent; then, assisted by Denis, succeeded in getting Wotan back to the house. On arrival, Wotan had fainted, but now was feeling better, and swearing like a trooper.

Concluding from this that he was not at death's door, Dullac insisted on having a private conversation with him immediately.

The doctor made a grimace expressing disapproval, but Dullac found an ally in Wotan himself.

'Dullac's quite right. He and I have got to have a talk. Clear out, all of you! I'm feeling perfectly all right.'

Suddenly, there was an angry shout: it came from Denis, who was now on his feet. 'Perfectly all right! He's feeling perfectly all right! He dares to say he's feeling perfectly all right! Dyana! What about Dyana? Is she feeling perfectly all right? Who'll bring her back to me? Can't you see we're damned? That there's a curse on this house? No, he doesn't see anything! He wants to talk – and he's feeling "perfectly all right"!'

Then, apparently exhausted, he collapsed into his chair, buried his head in his hands and deep sobs broke the embarrassed silence in the room.

Finally, Wotan said, 'Take him away. Give him a sleeping-pill and get him back up to his flat. You'd better stay with him tonight, Claire, to keep an eye on him.'

He then proceeded to thank Wetzel and the doctor for their trouble, and they both promised to drop in and see him next morning. As soon as they had gone the two women led Denis gently away with maternal solicitude: by now he had the grace to look ashamed of himself.

'That boy's no son of mine,' Wotan declared bitterly.

'You shouldn't blame him,' Dullac said. 'When Dyana's murder is followed by tonight's attack on you, it's a lot for him to go through. What would you have done if, instead of Dyana, it had been Edwige who was killed?'

'I'd have taken things into my own hands,' Wotan said savagely. 'I'd have hunted down her murderer and strangled him.'

Dullac reflected that this might not be far from the truth. 'That's all very well, but you've got to face the fact that your son is different from you. In short, if you'll forgive my saying so, you should learn to tolerate people being made the way they are and realize that there's nothing you can do about it.'

'You're a well-meaning man, Dullac,' Wotan said after a moment's silence, 'but I find you very irritating. I'm quite aware of what people say about me. And I don't give a damn!'

Dullac let this pass. When he finally spoke, it was to ask, 'Grün . . . Who shot you tonight?'

'If only I knew.'

'But the point is: *you do know.*'

'What!'

'You do know,' Dullac repeated firmly. 'Who are you shielding? And why?'

'You're mad!' Wotan protested and, in his indignation, made a gesture that caused him to wince with pain.

'Keep calm or you'll start bleeding again. Someone's got a grudge against you and a strong enough one to make him want to kill you. Don't tell me you don't know who it is.'

'Lots of people have grudges against me.'

'Not strong enough ones to make them shoot you.'

'Do you think tonight's attack is tied up with Dyana's murder?'

'With the burglary, in any case; and as the burglary appears to be tied up with the murder . . . well, you must admit it's a reasonable inference.'

'Yes, but you're mistaken. I'm certain of that. I know you are.'

'Then it's obvious that you're hiding something from me,' Dullac said triumphantly. 'And I'll tell you what it is.'

'Oh, will you?' Grün retorted aggressively but, under the aggression Dullac thought he detected a distinct note of anxiety. He decided to take a chance.

'Tell me,' he said almost casually, 'how do you manage to fabricate your gold?'

'*What's that you're saying!?*' Wotan sat up straight on the sofa. Caught off his guard, he was unable to control his expression, and Dullac could read in it both confusion and anger. Then Grün fell back again and asked sharply, 'Who on earth came up with that story?'

'You don't imagine I'm going to tell you!'

'It's just gossip! Idiotic gossip! It's impossible to transmute lead. I've never succeeded in doing it.'

'Then you have tried?'

'Yes, I'll admit that. It amused me to try out formulas I'd read in certain old books. But they never came to anything, needless to say.'

'What about your gold leaf?'

'I buy it, my friend! I buy it! I can show you the receipts. Whatever made you believe such nonsense?'

'I didn't believe you'd fabricated gold. But I was convinced you'd tried to.'

'Merely for amusement, as I just told you.'

'No! Not for amusement! You really believed it could be done! You still do! So don't tell me it was just a hobby. *It's the great project of your life.* And you've recently discovered something, haven't you? A book that's brought some new light to the problem?'

Wotan did not answer, but sweat was pouring down his face, and Dullac realized he was on the right track. Suddenly, he had an inspiration. 'Well, I'm damned! The *incunabulum!*'

'Go to the devil!' Wotan roared at him.

'And that explains the burglary! On Thursday evening, during the meeting, the conversation turned to gold and you spoke about your book of spells, the transmutation of lead and the Philosopher's Stone. I imagine the *incunabulum* was in the room within your friends' reach, since you're very proud of it and like to display it. Any one of the people present could have leafed through it, and, as they're all well-educated, deciphered it. Don't you see? *I believe someone did decipher it!*'

Grün made no comment, and Dullac went on, 'The person in question read enough of it to decide that the *incunabulum* was well worth stealing. And that same night he stole it! He took other books of spells and some of your gold leaf, too, to put us off the scent, but also because the books might contain additional information. That explains the hurried, amateurish nature of the theft. It was carried out on the spur of the moment without any previous planning. Now, tell me . . . Who went up to the *incunabulum* during the meeting?'

'Lots of people,' Wotan snapped, abandoning any further denials. 'Do you imagine I haven't been flogging my memory since last Friday morning?'

'And you can't recall seeing the *incunabulum* being leafed through at one time or another?'

'That, yes.'

'By whom?' When Dullac got no answer, he persisted, 'By whom, Grün?'

Grün still remained silent and Dullac suddenly lost his temper. 'You're so naïve! That's what you are, naïve! You think they're your friends, don't you? Your good, loyal friends? Well, do you know what they've said about you, those friends of yours? How they've described you to me?'

'Not all of them!'

'Yes! All of them.'

'Not Wetzel!' Grün shouted, but a moment later bit his lip.

'Wetzel!' Dullac said, enlightened. 'Good, honest, loyal Wetzel! He was the one looking through the *incunabulum*, wasn't he?'

'Yes, I did see him doing it, but it doesn't prove anything. Others could have done it, too. Did do it. If there's anyone in the discussion group I trust completely, it's Wetzel.'

'I must admit he's the only one who spoke of you with any warmth. So what? When one's own interests are involved, friendship doesn't count for much. And now I come to think of it, he'd already tried to buy up your business.'

'Ah, he told you that, did he? Well, it's true enough, but

he only made the offer to help me out. And when a fortunate sale put me back on my feet, there were no hard feelings on his part: he was delighted for my sake.'

'All the same, I notice he wasn't with you at the Weberstub on Thursday evening. Actually, when it comes to the burglary, the only people who have alibis are those who were in your party till half-past two in the morning: that's to say, the two psychiatrists, Boersen and Madame de Potztausend.'

Grün smiled. 'I can't really see Alice as a burglar.'

Dullac smiled, too. 'No, even if she hadn't an alibi, I think we could eliminate her. But where were all the others after the meeting broke up? At home, they say. But they've nothing to prove it. I shall have to go into their alibis for Thursday night again as well as their alibis for tonight.' He found the prospect depressing.

'All the same, you don't really think it was Wetzel who shot me?'

'I don't think anything. I confine myself to ascertaining the facts.'

'Facts!' Wotan flung at him with immense contempt.

'Yes, facts, and here's one of them for you to consider: just now, your friend Wetzel came running up immediately the shot was fired.'

'Nothing sinister about that. He lives only a few steps away.'

'Quite! But what is rather odd is that he was fully dressed from head to foot. If he'd been at home as he claims, he'd have been in comfortable indoor clothes.'

'It wasn't even ten o'clock. You could hardly have expected him to be in his pyjamas and dressing-gown.'

'If he'd come out in his slippers, trousers and waistcoat, I wouldn't have thought twice. But to see him in his outdoor shoes and jacket did surprise me.'

'You're talking nonsense,' Wotan growled. 'I'm not a complete fool. If the man's friendliness had just been a pretence I'd have felt it, known it. And Florence is devoted to me.'

'Ah, yes, there's Florence . . . ' Dullac said thoughtfully.

'Believe me, Superintendent, you're on the wrong track if you suspect Wetzel.'

'Then, who was it, Grün? . . . Tell me who it was.'

But there was no answer from Grün.

TUESDAY

1

At nine o'clock on Tuesday morning Holz was in Dullac's office making his report.

'Following your instructions, I went to see young Wilfrid-Hamlet Boersen. He's a very good type. Conscientious student, neat appearance, doesn't sleep around. Hopes to be a diplomat like his father.'

'What did he have to say?'

'He also confirmed the timing, first at the meeting and then at the Weberstub. He admires Wotan very much, though I'm not sure it's entirely disinterested.'

'What's he got to gain?'

'I think he wants to make the right contacts in Strasbourg. Looking to the future.'

'Ambitious chap, is he?'

'You can say that again!'

'I see. What did you make of Charles Feldmann?'

'A different type of student altogether. Younger – only twenty – shy, awkward and given to blushing; probably a virgin. Has the beginnings of a beard. Friend of Denis's at the university and outside it: shares his views. Last Thursday Denis had dinner with him at half-past seven. At ten o'clock he wanted to go home, and Charles walked back with him to the Place Benjamin-Zix, where they separated.'

'That confirms Denis's story,' Dullac observed.

'Yes, but from the time he left Denis Grün Feldmann hasn't an alibi. He says he walked straight home and went to bed. Now, Dyana Pasquier was murdered between midnight and two o'clock.'

'I can't really see what motive Charles Feldmann could have had to murder Dyana Pasquier,' Dullac said. But, at the same time, he remembered something that bothered him: a short sentence of Father Doppelleben's. 'Apart from young Schwarz,' the priest had said, 'the members of the discussion group had no apparent contact with Dyana.' It was the word 'apparent' that nagged at him. Who was to know whether Dyana hadn't been secretly on intimate terms with one of the witnesses? And, if she had, why not with Charles Feldmann? And why not with the Pope? he asked himself angrily. Aloud, he asked Holz, 'Did you manage to get in touch with Schiller's friend, Roland Berthet?'

'Yes, I rang him up.'

'And?'

'He confirmed that Schiller was in Colmar all Thursday evening and the following night.'

'Colmar . . . ' Dullac said, frowning. 'Colmar's cropped up several times. But in connection with what? And whom?'

'So many things have cropped up,' Holz said sympathetically. 'Don't worry, Chief. It'll come back to you if you don't think too hard.'

'Let's hope so. Anyway, we've got all the statements in writing by now. I'll go through them carefully this evening at home. What else?'

'The two Androses . . . '

'Ah! Yes.'

'The daughter, Abigail, was with her father, so I was able to kill two birds with one stone. I saw Germain Andros in his office . . . '

'First things first!' Dullac interrupted. 'Tell me about the show.'

'Beautiful, Chief! Really beautiful! It started with an overture from one of Wagner's operas and the whole theatre full of smoke. A lot of people had coughing-fits but that didn't really matter. As soon as the programme girls had opened the doors again to ventilate the auditorium, the curtain went up. And what scenery! The Rhine, spot on. Its steep, rocky banks took up the whole of the back of the stage, with real sand and real rocks. On the left was the Lorelei rock full-size; on the right, also full-size, Strasbourg Cathedral in sections: the sacristy with all the sacred vessels and vestments, the great nave, the altar and the stained-glass windows; in the centre, the Rhine with real water which a hydraulic system collected at the bottom and took back to the top so that it could flow down again; and on the Rhine, the ferry-boat with its oarsmen. The whole accompanied by incidental music, birdsong and the sound of flowing water. Terrific!'

'Must have been,' Dullac said, fascinated. 'What was the play actually about?'

'Haven't the faintest. The sound-effects drowned the actors' voices and there was so much to look at one forgot to listen.'

'Well, what was the play called?'

'*Huis-Clos*, Chief. It was written by someone called Sartre.'

'I hope you congratulated Germain Andros warmly?'

'Yes, I started off by doing that. Then I came to the point and asked the questions we're interested in; not that I learned anything sensational. Father and daughter, like everyone else, confirmed the timetable for Thursday evening and the row between Claire and her father. On the off-chance I mentioned young Schwarz's name and Mademoiselle Andros immediately blushed and looked away.'

'He seems to be a great success with the ladies,' Dullac commented; just then a uniformed policeman came in to say that Daniel Schwarz was waiting to see him: 'He said he'd been told to come.'

'That's right. Show him in.'

When Schwarz appeared, he turned out to be a good-looking young man in his early twenties, slim and broad-shouldered, with long hair which he wore like a halo, immediately calling to mind one of Raphael's apostles. But there was nothing angelic about his face: his aquiline nose, and square, determined chin were more suggestive of virility and energy.

Dullac greeted him pleasantly and asked him to sit down. 'I imagine you know why I've asked you to come and see me?'

'I've read the papers,' Schwarz said laconically.

'I'm afraid it may be painful for you to . . . '

Schwarz broke in, 'Just ask me whatever questions you want, Superintendent, and I'll do my best to answer them.'

'Well, it's rather a delicate matter . . . I very much admired the portrait you did of Mademoiselle Pasquier and . . . '

'And you're tactfully trying to find out if I was in love with her? I was.'

Dullac was impressed. The young man's seriousness and self-control brought Martine back to his mind. Here, too, was someone suffering from genuine grief, and, like her, being at pains not to display it. With his dignity, strength of character and talent, he gave promise of becoming a first-class painter, and a man to be reckoned with.

'As you seem to appreciate that I'm only doing my duty, I'll come straight to the point. What was your exact relationship with Mademoiselle Pasquier?'

'We were just good friends, and I mean precisely that. We never slept together. I told her how I felt about her, and she said she was very touched by it, but she was in love with Denis Grün, and it was no good my cherishing any hopes. That didn't mean that we couldn't go on seeing each other as often as we wanted to, and I could go on telling her I adored her if that gave me any pleasure.'

'Wasn't that rather dangerous for her?'

'No. She was far too much attached to Denis. I was her page, that's all.'

Her page! It was the same word that Jacques Schiller had employed to describe his relationship with Claire, Dullac reflected. The young men in Claire's and Dyana's set seemed to share the same romantic outlook. Dismissing this thought, which he found vaguely disturbing, he continued his interrogation. 'Was it before or after you'd expressed your feelings for her that you painted her portrait?'

'After. I did it six months ago.'

'Oh, quite recently, then?'

'Yes. I remember I was doing it when that business . . .'

'What business?'

'A bit of a row between the members of the discussion group.'

'Yes, I've heard about that. It seems you were on the side of Wotan's opponents?'

'That's true, I was. I didn't approve of Madame de Potztausend's motives, but the Pastor and his wife clearly had nothing but the good of the discussion group at heart. And they were quite right. Wotan's apt to think he's God Almighty, and that's unhealthy.'

'What's your frank opinion of him?'

'Not very favourable, I'm afraid. He's certainly a picturesque old character and sometimes quite engaging. But what an egotist! And how determined to take charge of everything! And what absurd family pride! Dyana suffered a lot from it.'

'How?'

'Wotan and Denis didn't agree about anything except that they both had this worship of the Grün family. When Dyana met Denis four years ago she looked after him in every way, financially and otherwise. That lasted for a year until he got his grant. You'd have thought that the Grüns might have shown some gratitude towards her for all she did for him during that period, but not a bit of it! It was the least she could have done: nothing was too good for Monsieur Denis, the great intellectual, the armchair revolutionary! Do you know what Charles Feldmann had the nerve to say about Dyana once? "All right, so she gets very tired. But it's what she wants. After all, there are other harder and less well-paid jobs." That's what Monsieur Grün junior's friends thought of Dyana!'

'I see you don't care for him much!'

'I don't. I admit I'm prejudiced; but who wouldn't be in my place?'

Dullac nodded. 'I understand your feelings. Thank you for coming: I don't think I've anything further to ask you . . . Oh, yes, there is one thing. What did you do last Thursday after the meeting broke up?'

'I drove back home.'

'To Ingwiller?'

'Yes.'

'That's some thirty kilometres from here. What time did you get back?'

'My car's an old second-hand one. I must have taken three-quarters of an hour.'

'Then we can say between a quarter- and half-past eleven?'

'About that, yes.'

'Did you see anyone when you got there?'

'No. My parents were sound asleep, and there was no one about in the village.'

'Thank you. If I should think of anything else, perhaps you'd be good enough to come here again?'

'Whenever you like,' Schwarz said politely and left.

As soon as he was out of earshot, Dullac asked Holz, 'Well, what do you think? He could be our man, couldn't he? Impetuous, very much in love, unhappy . . . and no alibi!'

'I suppose he might have killed Dyana in a fit of despair, but why shoot Grün?'

'To avenge his beloved! In his opinion, the Grüns persecuted her.'

'That would mean our assuming that he's mentally unbalanced . . . '

'Which doesn't tally with our impression of him . . . Now let's turn to something else.'

'What?'

'The disappearance and reappearance of the body. One always comes back to that. Why should anyone take the body out of the river and put it in the workroom?'

'We've assumed it was to harm the Grüns. But the only thing I feel certain of is that the three affairs are linked together – the burglary, Dyana's murder, and the attempt to kill Wotan. It would mean too many coincidences otherwise.'

'All right, let's start from there and follow our friend Loiseau's practice; examine the alibis on one hand and the motives on the other.'

'Taking the alibis, Denis was with Loiseau between midnight and two o'clock, the period during which the crime was committed. Could Loiseau have been his accomplice?'

'Don't be an idiot, Holz! Loiseau's record in the force was impeccable.'

'Then it would have been physically impossible for Denis to have committed the murder. Pity.'

'That last word is quite uncalled-for!'

'I withdraw it, Chief,' Holz said promptly. 'Particularly as Denis seems to be eliminated as well by the absence of any motive.'

'Dyana was pressing him to marry her, and he didn't want to.'

'Not much of a motive. Besides, from what Martine Blitz told you, Dyana seems to have been on his side recently.'

'Forget him. Anyone can see that he's heartbroken: there's no question of him putting on an act. Who's next?'

'Wotan Grün. He's got an unbreakable alibi, too. From eleven o'clock till after two o'clock, fifty people saw him at the Weberstub. All the statements agree.'

'We could adjust the time a little,' Dullac said without conviction. 'The pathologist puts two o'clock as the final limit. Suppose we extend it to half-past two, a quarter to three? Wotan goes home with his wife and daughter, then, when they're in bed, goes out again and drowns Dyana close to the house.'

'But what would she be doing close to the house? There are only two possibilities: either the murderer met her by pure chance walking along the river bank – and that rules out premeditation; or he'd made an appointment with her.'

'That's so. What's more, it's clear that Dyana couldn't have been drowned where Madame Dickbauch found her, because there's nowhere to walk at that spot, and the foot-bridge is two metres above the water: so the murder must have been committed somewhere upstream and the body carried down there by the current.'

'And there's still another thing, Chief. You're

stretching the time-limit much too far. As you'll remember, the experts said; between midnight and two o'clock, but probably between half-past twelve and half-past one. Now, Wotan didn't leave the Weberstub before half-past two!'

'And, finally, if we assume that the three affairs are linked, Wotan can scarcely have fired a shot at himself!'

'Scarcely . . . Do they know the type of weapon?'

'The bullet's been found in the stone of the parapet, and our boys have been dragging the river for the weapon: the murderer may have got rid of it there.'

'That's Denis and Wotan ruled out. Who's next?'

'Edwige,' Dullac said. 'She didn't like Dyana.'

'If one went about killing everyone one didn't like . . . '

'A very profound observation, Holz. Besides, Edwige has an alibi. From eleven o'clock onwards she was at the Weberstub. The same goes for Claire. And Schiller was in Colmar. But there's another good reason why none of the Grüns can reasonably be suspected.'

'What is it?'

'*The fact that the body was shifted!*'

Holz gave his superior an admiring look; then admitted sheepishly, 'I don't understand.'

'Don't you see, the murderer *wanted* the Grüns to be suspected? There's no other way to explain why the body was shifted. Here's a chap who has no idea that he's left marks on his victim's neck. He's confident that her death will be put down to accident or suicide. He's only got to let the body drift away and go home. But, instead of that, what does he do? He chases after the body, which the current no doubt swept out of his hands, and, when he finds it, deposits it in the workroom, thus providing us with *proof* that it's a case of murder. What matters to him is not that the death should be put down to an accident but that the Grüns shall be had up on a murder charge!'

'But you've forgotten that, in the meantime, Madame Dickbauch and twenty other people have seen the body in the river. That spoils any chance of his trick succeeding.'

'I haven't forgotten it. *But the murderer never knew it!* Assume that the murder was committed a considerable distance upstream. When the murderer reaches the spot where the body ended up, the witnesses will have been warming themselves up in Gräber's bar for some time; so he has no way of knowing it has been seen in the water. And it's a wonderful stroke of luck for him to find it trapped by the weeds so close to the Grüns' house!'

'Marvellous, Chief!' Holz said, genuinely impressed. 'But that means that everyone who was in Gräber's bar that night is in the clear.'

'Yes, unless . . . '

'Unless what?'

'Unless the murderer had an accomplice.'

Both men remained silent for a moment as the same name came to their minds. Finally, Holz observed, 'Mademoiselle Wetzel is a good athlete, isn't she?'

'A very good athlete. Strong, too.'

'And in love with Denis Grün.'

'Yes. And her father very keen to take over the shop and workroom.'

'To which, Edwige told us, she has the keys.'

'Making it unnecessary to break in.'

'We've got the motive and the opportunity, Chief.'

'So it seems . . . '

There was another silence and, once again, it was Holz who broke it. 'But if their object was to frame Grün, what was the point of the burglary?'

'It would be well worth their while.'

'You mean, the transmutation of lead? Do you really believe in it?'

'Wetzel may have believed in it.'

'All the same, the burglary cleared the Grüns.'

'Not necessarily. Don't you remember you thought Wotan might have faked it for the insurance money?'

'Yes, I did. They're a cunning pair! Couldn't have planned it more neatly. And we haven't a vestige of proof.'

'We'll dig some up,' Dullac said, then frowned. 'I wonder . . . What was it that was bothering me just now?'

He racked his brain for several minutes, then suddenly exclaimed, 'Damnation!' with such force that Holz jumped.

'What's wrong?'

'Everything! It can't have been the Wetzels.'

'Why not?'

'We're crazy! Don't you see? Wetzel was there when Madame Dickbauch spotted the body! And our whole theory rests on the fact that the murderer wasn't aware of it.'

'His daughter didn't know. It was she who put the body in the workroom.'

'But her father would have been able to warn her! Stop her making the blunder. He wasn't compelled to go to the bar with Madame Dickbauch and the others. He could have slipped away.'

Holz groaned. 'You're right!'

'Yes, unfortunately.'

'And now we've got to start all over again from the beginning.'

'Afraid so.'

'And it all fitted together so well!'

'Except I've just proved it didn't!'

'Then who can it be? The Pastor? One doesn't go to those lengths just because of a trifling disagreement. Madame de Potztausend? Disappointed in love, she wants to be revenged on Wotan? It's too laughable! The two psychiatrists? A sudden attack of madness?'

'That's your best theory to date,' Dullac said gravely.

'All the same, it's a bit far-fetched. Besides, they've got an alibi: they were at the Weberstub with the Grüns.'

'Someone's making monkeys of us, Holz!'

'Yes, but who? Dammit, who?'

'Abigail Andros,' Dullac said promptly.

'Abigail Andros? Why on earth?'

'I don't know. Because she's the least likely suspect.'

'Now you're laughing at me, Chief!' Holz protested.

'Not at you; at myself. Because I haven't got anywhere. I'm just as much in the dark as when I started. Yet I'm certain all the clues are there right under our noses in the statements we've been given. It's up to us to have the intelligence to spot them. If only there were something . . . the smallest incident . . . a new fact . . . '

Before he could finish the sentence the telephone rang.

2

Wotan Grün was sobbing. Without restraint or self-consciousness. His face buried in his arms, his powerful shoulders shaking convulsively; indifferent, for once, to what anyone might think of him and, for once, genuinely noble in his grief, noble as he had never appeared before. He was sobbing in great gasps, and everyone around him, frozen with pity and horror but even more amazement, watched unbelievingly the giant's total collapse.

Edwige, Claire, and the faithful Wetzel, white as sheets, were completely at a loss. Anything could happen. Anything! But that Wotan Grün should be crying was impossible, shocking and unnatural!

But what did it matter to him what they thought? What would life itself matter to him from now on? Up there in the loft that dominated the whole of Strasbourg, under the impassive eye of the ancestor in his frame, the body of his son was growing cold.

It was Claire once again who had summoned Dullac; it was she, too, who had opened the front door to him; and now, like her father, she was crying. She was doing so without any sound or sobs, that was the only difference; but without any more reserve than Wotan. How touching she was like this, Dullac thought. How much more attractive in her real weakness, in her little girl's forlornness, than in that cynical woman's mask which she normally assumed. If they had been alone he would have taken her into his arms.

It was Edwige who took charge. She preceded Dullac, Holz and the other police officers up to the second floor: the trap-door was open and the ladder down. She explained that Denis had been missing since morning and that they had immediately feared the worst; the act of despair that each of them had subconsciously expected. They had hunted for him everywhere; finally, Loiseau had thought of the loft; and they had rushed up there.

But too late. Denis was hanging from one of the main beams. On the floor, just below his feet, there was a small piece of paper, on which he had written, 'I can't go on. Goodbye. Forgive me.'

Nothing had been touched. Dullac ordered the body to be cut down and put in Denis's bedroom. Through the windows of the loft Strasbourg was proudly shining under the ironic rays of the immortal sun. Dullac thought back to the time, a day or so before, when the landscape had enchanted him: today he couldn't have cared less about it. Nor was he greatly concerned about this miserable death – at last he had picked up the scent.

He gave further orders: he wanted the autopsy report as quickly as possible. And let the lab boys and the handwriting experts get busy on the farewell note. He must have facts, not conjectures.

Not that it was really all that important. He was confident that his hunch was right. All the details were not yet clear: he required a little more time to think, alone in the privacy of his flat. He must put in a call to Colmar. Merely from conscientiousness: he already knew what the answer would be. And all this because of one small detail. A stupid, unnecessary grain of sand in the brilliant piece of machinery the murderer had constructed.

From a drawer in an old cupboard Holz had removed a packet of letters, tied up with a blue ribbon. All the letters had been written by the same person, and that person was not Wotan Grün. And all of them began with the words, 'My adorable, my beloved, my darling Edwige . . . '

WEDNESDAY

'Chief! They've found the gun!'

'In the river, I suppose?'

'Yes. And do you know what it is?'

'A high-precision rifle with telescopic sights.'

'Good Lord, Chief, how did you guess? You're the devil in person!'

'No, Holz. Not me. In this affair, the devil definitely isn't me.'

'All the same . . . ' Holz began, then broke off as a policeman came in with the gun. 'Ah, he's brought you the rifle.'

'Very efficient weapon,' Dullac commented. 'Doesn't it suggest anything to you?'

'Unfortunately, I haven't got your gift of second sight. Still, there's one thing you certainly won't have foreseen!'

'Something sensational?'

'And how! It concerns that piece of paper – Denis's farewell note.'

'It isn't his writing?'

'Yes, it's his all right. The handwriting experts are quite definite about that. So are the Grüns. Only the lab boys are quite definite, too.'

'And what have they got to say?' Dullac asked patiently.

'*That it was written over three years ago!*'

When Dullac made no comment, Holz insisted, 'Now

that does surprise you, doesn't it?'

'Not all that much.'

'You mean you suspected it?'

'I feared it.'

'But do you realize what it means? Denis Grün didn't commit suicide. *He was murdered!*'

'That seems the logical conclusion.'

'What I can't understand is where the note came from. Because it's Denis's all right: there's no doubt about that.'

'I can tell you where it came from. I rang up Loiseau this morning and asked him a number of questions. It appears that, when he saw Dyana rush away that night, she was carrying her handbag.'

'So?'

'When her body was found, the bag had disappeared.'

'Yes, but that's not surprising. The current would have carried it away.'

'Not at all. It was the murderer who took it. And do you know what he found in the bag?'

'No.'

'He found the farewell letter that Denis wrote to Dyana three years ago when they had a row, the one Martine told me Dyana always kept in her bag. And do you know what Denis wrote to Dyana at that time?'

'No.'

'The letter began with the words: "Dearest Dyana. I can't go on. Goodbye. Forgive me." '

'Well, I'm damned!'

'The letter went on in much the same way. But the murderer only had to cut out the words that served his purpose, and that was that – everyone would think that Denis

Grün had committed suicide, leaving a note behind that
put the matter beyond any doubt.'

'But he hadn't reckoned with our experts . . . '

'No. Very useful fellows . . . By the way, don't make
any engagements for tomorrow night. We're going out.'

'Both of us?'

'Yes. Tomorrow's Thursday. We've been invited to the
meeting of Wotan Grün's discussion group.'

THURSDAY

1

Never before had there been so many people at a meeting of Wotan's discussion group; and never before had the meeting assumed such a curious character.

At first everyone had been baffled. The whole of Strasbourg was talking about nothing but Denis's murder and Wotan's deep despair; yet, on Wednesday afternoon or Thursday morning, all the members of the group had received a telephone call or a telegram from Edwige and Claire, bidding them to come to the meeting as usual.

Later on, they began to guess what was brewing. It could not, of course, have been the Grüns' invitation: it must really have been Dullac's. Which meant that the mystery surrounding Dyana's and Denis's deaths must have come close to being solved. This theory became a certainty when the regulars at the Thursday meetings observed that their numbers had been augmented by the unaccustomed presence of Noel Loiseau, Martine Blitz, Jacques Schiller, Charles Feldmann, Roland Berthet and – surprise, surprise! – Pastor Michelon and his wife.

But what provoked the greatest astonishment was the presence of Wotan Grün, a huge, tragic figure wrapped in a formidable silence. His face was inscrutable, completely impassive. It seemed as though nothing could stir or move him any more; and, confronted by the unquestionable

authenticity of his grief, the silence devoid of any affecta-
tion, and the black velvet suit that he had put on without
any desire to parade his sorrow, but simply as a tribute to
the son he had lost, everyone realized that, in stripping
him of his second-rate actor's mask and his trumpery
grandeur, misfortune had endowed the last of the Grüns
with a genuine nobility.

When everyone had arrived and sat down – Inspector
Holz occupying a seat close to the door – Dullac, standing
alone in the middle of the room, suddenly felt a wave of
pride sweep over him. Self-confident, his praiseworthy
efforts crowned with success, he did not look at Claire, but
felt the young woman's attention concentrated on him,
which provided a further source of satisfaction as he began
his speech:

'Ladies and gentlemen, I asked our friend Wotan Grün,
despite the cruel blows he has recently suffered, to allow
us all to meet here tonight. It is exactly a week ago today
that Dyana was found dead, murdered in mysterious
circumstances that left us with a difficult problem to solve.
During the week I proceeded in the dark, sticking stakes in
at random in the hope of marking a route. Today, those
stakes have borne fruit.'

Total silence enveloped the room, and the tension
among his audience was such that it did not occur to any
of them that stakes were not fruit-bearing.

Dullac went on, 'In addition to the routine questions,
Who? Why? How? two subsidiary ones immediately
arose: why had the body been moved? And had the burglary any connection with the murder?

'The answer to the first question occurred to me almost

at once: the murderer wanted to focus attention on the Grüns' house. Unaware that the body had been seen by several witnesses when it was lying in the river, he thought he would divert suspicion on to one or other of the Grün family. To his dismay, the plan recoiled on himself: if the murderer had been one of the Grüns, he would have left the body where it was instead of moving it into the house. In any case, his luck was dead out: all the Grüns had cast-iron alibis.

'Having settled that point, I was left with the second question. I answered that one quickly, too, and in the affirmative. For the burglary and the murder to have occurred on the same day, at the same time and in the same place purely by coincidence was too improbable. So now one was faced with interpreting the connection. Had the burglary been committed in order to distract our attention from the murder by suggesting that Dyana Pasquier had caught the burglar in the act? Or should we conclude that the murder and burglary were complementary, two facets of the same plan? But what was the plan? If its only object was to steal some rare books and a small quantity of gold leaf, what need was there to kill? Altogether, the burglary was an unusual one: the murderer had made no attempt to get into the shop or force the safe. There were two possible explanations for this: either it was because the burglary was only staged to deceive us; or because the murderer had immediately found what he'd come for in the workroom. Now, what was there in the workroom? Only a minute part of the gold leaf: the rest was in the safe. So it must have been the books he was after. The problem then was to find out what common interest could be served in stealing the books and killing Dyana Pasquier.

'I was completely at a loss for a long time. Then, last Monday, Martine Blitz supplied me with some material for an answer. But I found it quite extraordinary. According to her, Dyana Pasquier and Claire Grün had told her in confidence that Wotan Grün had been trying to fabricate gold, had perhaps even succeeded; in any case, was close to achieving it. And the secret, that fabulous secret, had apparently been hidden in an old book, no doubt one of those that had been stolen, most probably the *incunabulum*. I must admit I was sceptical, but the murderer might have been naïve enough to believe in the impossible, and want to get his hands on the magic spells.

'If this were so, I now knew the motive for the burglary. As regards the motive for the murder, it was self-evident, since I'd adopted the theory that the two crimes were linked together. Dyana knew the identity of the murderer, might even have been his accomplice; in any case, she had been killed to make certain she did not talk. This appeared to be confirmed by the mysterious hint she had given her friend, Martine: "One of these days I'll tell you something," and also by the fact that she had seemed recently to be unusually excited.

'But, parallel with this, I'd heard another story, this time from several witnesses: that six months ago, Wotan Grün's discussion group had been shaken by a minor palace revolution, and, while some members had loyally supported him, others had rebelled against a dictatorship they regarded as uncalled-for and excessive.'

Dullac broke off to glance at the people surrounding

him. The members of the group were exchanging embarrassed, furtive looks, and fidgeting in their seats. Finally, Alice de Potztausend spoke up. 'But, my dear Monsieur Dullac, surely I'm right in saying that each of us explained our views on the subject to you very frankly?'

'Yes, that's so,' Dullac agreed, 'but the fact remains that the incident revealed that not all Wotan Grün's friends were devoted to him, and that they wouldn't have minded hurting him. And who can tell whether those who appeared to be the most loyal to him were not merely good actors?'

There was an uneasy murmur round the room. Smiling, Dullac waited for it to die down, then continued, 'I confess that there were certain members of the group to whom I could not attribute the slightest motive. For instance, Monsieur and Mademoiselle Andros and Monsieur Boersen. The two Gruaus were given to announcing that Wotan Grün was mentally unbalanced, but I soon discovered that they thought the same about almost everyone else.'

'Let me tell you . . . !' Madame Gruau shouted, getting to her feet; then, when Dullac attempted to interrupt her, changed what she had been going to say to, 'We certainly shan't stay here any longer to be insulted! Isn't that so, Gilbert?'

'Yes, dear,' said a voice from the furthest corner of the room.

With her husband in her wake Janine headed for the door, but came up against a smiling Holz, who politely conducted her back to her seat.

'Then there were Pastor and Madame Michelon,'

Dullac resumed. 'They represented the more thoughtful element in the small coalition, and they could not provide any alibi; all the same, I couldn't see them setting out to steal an *incunabulum*, and, still less, to murder Dyana!'

'Thank you, Monsieur Dullac,' the Pastor murmured.

'In the case of Monsieur Wetzel and his daughter, there were more grounds for suspicion. Last year, the father had wanted to take over the Grüns' shop and workroom; Florence, for her part, had a crush on Denis and could have regarded Dyana as a rival. However, some rather intricate reasoning by Inspector Holz and myself enabled us to rule them out. Unlike the villains in detective stories, the Wetzels were not putting on an act; their friendship for the Grüns was entirely genuine.'

'You may have doubted it,' said a voice. 'I never did.'

The gathering experienced a moment of emotion. The deep, harsh voice belonged to Wotan Grün, speaking for the first time that evening. And it had been raised in defence of a friend!

Wetzel's eyes were clouded with tears as he softly said, 'Thank you, Wotan.'

'Now, who was there left?' Dullac continued. 'Madame de Potztausend nursed very warm feelings for the head of the Grün family: on the death of his first wife, she had hoped for a time that . . . '

'What on earth are you talking about, young man?' the poetess demanded indignantly. 'You're wandering! That's how history comes to be written!' she added, gazing round her for sympathy and support. When she failed to detect any, she looked deeply hurt and lapsed into silence.

'However, I ruled her out,' Dullac proceeded. 'I judged her to be perfectly capable of assassinating someone, but only through the medium of her poetry. I passed on to Daniel Schwarz, who had very much impressed me. He was passionately in love with Dyana Pasquier; he had painted her portrait and she had confided in him; he made no secret of his dislike for the Grüns, and he hadn't an alibi. But I trust in my ability to sum men up: he could never have raised a hand against Dyana. That left me with just one more person.'

Dullac turned to face the Catholic priest, who asked pleasantly, 'Am I to understand, Superintendent, that you suspect me of homicide, that's to say of breaking Our Lord's holy law: "Thou shalt not kill"?'

'Unfortunately, Father, it has been known. But it's certainly not the case here. What I'm concerned with is certain facts you disclosed to me, relating to someone who's with us now.'

'My son!' the priest exclaimed, horrified. 'Those facts were gleaned from confidences entrusted to me. Remember that my honour and that of the person in question are at stake.'

'The trouble is, Father, that I found those facts considerably more illuminating than the pathetic little squabble between members of the discussion group. And I suddenly began to have doubts. Doubts about everything. I'd been made a fool of. Been lured into believing that the moon was made of green cheese. Alchemy? The Philosopher's Stone? The transmutation of lead into gold? Forget about them! It was a completely different secret that Dyana found herself sharing. Yours, madame,' he said, turning towards Edwige, whose face slowly drained of colour as she waited for what was to come.

Once again, Wotan's deep voice broke in. 'Mind what you're doing, Dullac!'

'I'm taking my revenge,' Dullac retorted. 'Teaching people it doesn't pay to take me for a fool. This, in brief, is what I learnt from Father Doppelleben: a year ago, Madame Grün fell for a man who was very much in love with her. She remained faithful to her husband, but, from that moment on, her whole life was transformed.' He swung round to face Jacques Schiller's friend. 'Monsieur Berthet, you live in Colmar, don't you? The town in which Edwige Grün grew up?'

A deathly silence followed his question. When he finally answered, Berthet was as pale as Edwige. 'I suppose you think you're doing your duty, Superintendent. It's your only possible excuse. But you're making a great mistake. You're presuming that I killed Dyana to keep her quiet, then burgled the workroom to avert suspicion: all that just because Edwige had confided in her. Well, you're utterly wrong. Because I was never – do you hear me? – never Edwige Grün's lover. And Dyana, who knew the whole story, knew that, too.'

'You'll have difficulty in proving it,' Dullac snapped, then added with a slight smile that somehow made his expression even more alarming, 'Unless, of course, you can produce an alibi for the night of the murder.'

'No, I haven't got an alibi, but . . .'

'You haven't? That's interesting. *Then your friend Jacques Schiller wasn't staying with you?*'

'What I meant was . . .'

'Too late! You've given yourself away. And you've given him away too. Your generosity can't save him any longer.'

'It wasn't me,' Jacques stammered. 'It isn't true!'

'You weren't Edwige's lover?' Dullac demanded in a voice of thunder and produced the packet of letters from his pocket. 'Then what about these letters – love letters – which were found in the loft, and have your signature on them?'

Jacques did not answer. He stared vacantly at the letters for a moment, then crouched forward in his chair, sobbing like a desolate child.

Grün could be heard stifling a groan. Two days earlier he would have killed Jacques on the spot: today all he could do was groan.

'I'd noticed a contradiction, Monsieur Schiller,' Dullac went on. 'You led me to believe that you had no great liking for Edwige Grün, whereas Martine Blitz told me that you admired her. So you'd lied to me. You were Edwige's lover. After your friend Berthet had told you in confidence of his short platonic affair with her, you decided to try your own luck. And taking advantage of her confused state of mind at the time, you succeeded in seducing her. You were both happy to let Dyana in on your secret until you realized that she was a potential danger to you. She may even have tried to blackmail you. This explains – in another way – Dyana's hint to Martine Blitz: "One of these days I'll tell you something . . . " You then carefully worked out a plan. Berthet agreed to provide you with an alibi, half because of his friendship for you and Edwige, half because your knowledge of his own affair with her gave you a hold over him. Edwige was your accomplice. Before leaving for the Weberstub she left the shop and workroom doors unlocked. Claire, for her part, loved you enough to stifle her jealousy and back up your alibi by pretending to have rung you in Colmar. Very sporting of you, Claire!' Dullac added bitterly. 'You must have loved your page very much to risk prison for his sake!'

'I did love him, that's quite true,' Claire admitted coolly. 'But it's all over now. He deceived my father and he deceived me.'

'And when I think . . . !' Dullac burst out in a fury. 'When I think that he had the infernal nerve and the cynicism to tell me the truth to my face! And that I didn't catch on! "My alibi isn't worth anything, you know. Claire and I could have cooked up the whole story!" The bastard!'

Jacques was still sobbing with his head in his hands. All he could manage by way of reply was to mumble, 'It wasn't me! It wasn't me, I tell you. I didn't kill Dyana!'

'Oh yes you did!' Dullac insisted. 'Just as you tried to kill Wotan. And succeeded in killing Denis. Encouraged by your first success, you began to get big ideas. All you had to do was to get rid of the two Grüns, father and son, and you'd be left with the two women, the house and a fortune! Well, now you've got to pay. Do you realize what that means?'

'It wasn't me!' Jacques shouted. He looked up at Dullac, tears pouring down his face, and tried to grab the edge of his jacket with trembling, ineffectual hands. 'It's quite true – I admit it – that I've behaved abominably and been a bloody fool. I fell for Edwige and persuaded her to sleep with me. And I invented a false alibi and made a joke of it in front of you. But I'm not guilty of anything more than that. I swear it! I'll swear it on anything you like! Dyana was like a sister to me: I'd never have done anything to hurt her. I've never killed anyone in my life!'

Dullac's voice was suddenly gentle as he said, '*I'm aware of that, my boy.*'

If he had wanted to create a sensation, he could not have been more successful. His audience, who had been watching the poignant scene, sitting on the edges of their seats and convinced of young Schiller's guilt, could scarcely get over it. What a superb actor the Superintendent was!

Meanwhile the Superintendent went on, 'I'm well aware of it. And I suppose you'd like to know how. By the merest chance. Through a grain of sand that got into the machinery. The murderer missed out on one small detail; didn't know that on the first day I came here to start my investigations, *I went up to the loft.* And had already opened that all-important drawer. *Your letters weren't there!*

'Do you get the point? The letters were planted there later, with a view to my finding them and charging you with the murder. No, my boy, you've never killed anyone. And you didn't invent a false alibi for yourself: the idea was very cleverly suggested to you. And, in fact, it was for herself and not for you that the person in question arranged the alibi. *Isn't that so, Mademoiselle Claire?*'

There was a long, agonizing silence. Then Wotan's voice was heard. 'What are you insinuating, Dullac?'

'I'm not insinuating anything,' Dullac said calmly. 'I'm merely waiting for Claire's answer.'

'That won't take me long,' Claire retorted. 'You've just proved that I had no alibi between twenty to eleven and eleven. Well, may I remind you that Dyana was killed much later, between half-past twelve and half-past one? And that, during that period, I was at the Weberstub?'

'There's no point in trying to defend yourself, you know,' Dullac said, almost kindly. 'I've told you that I went up to the loft on Saturday morning. And I've told you that Jacques's letters weren't there then. But you must know that the rifle with telescopic sights *was* there.'

'You mean the weapon that was used to shoot my father?'

'Yes, that one.'

'How could I have guessed that it was? Anyone could have taken the gun.'

'From your own loft?'

'Then let's say, anyone in the house.'

'It wasn't anyone, Claire. It was you.'

'Prove it!'

In a voice of restrained grief, Wotan Grün intervened, 'Do you realize, Dullac, that you're actually accusing my daughter, my own daughter, of shooting me?'

'Why not? The two of you didn't get on so well together! It was a good idea, Claire, but it didn't come off. If only I hadn't gone up to the loft . . . But I did. It was fate. Your brother, perhaps, might have heard Holz, Loiseau and me manipulating the trap-door and ladder, but he was listening to *Rheingold*, and the music drowned the noise.'

'What difference would it have made if Denis had heard you?'

'He'd have warned you. You, his accomplice.'

'His accomplice!'

'Certainly. *Because it was your brother who killed Dyana, wasn't it, Claire?*'

'You're crazy, Dullac!' Loiseau suddenly burst out. 'Denis was with me almost all night. Or are you accusing me of being an accomplice, too?'

'Of course not, my dear Loiseau. But, like me, you were the victim of a very neat conjuring trick. A trick played on us by Denis Grün and Claire as his assistant. One little sentence in your statement, one little sentence that seemed quite unimportant, held the whole key to the mystery. In perfectly good faith you stated that Denis hadn't left you all night. But that wasn't absolutely correct. Because you also told me – I'm quoting from memory – "He insisted on showing me a letter that Dyana had written him . . . " Now, I don't suppose he had it on him, did he?'

'No, he didn't. He fetched it from his flat.'

'So he did leave you at that particular moment?'

'But only for a couple of minutes, my dear Dullac! Possibly three, but no more. He didn't have time in three minutes to go down two flights of stairs, run along the river bank until he found Dyana, drown her, and then come back up to my place, breathing perfectly normally, and without a drop of sweat.'

'Our mistake was in taking it for granted that she was drowned in the river.'

'Do you mean she wasn't?'

'Obviously not.'

'Then where was she drowned?'

'*At home. In her bath.*'

'In her bath?'

'It's the only solution,' Dullac said, as tongues began wagging all round him.

For a moment, Loiseau stared at him, completely confused; then he suddenly recovered and protested, 'No! No! It isn't possible! When Denis went back to his flat to fetch the letter, it was one o'clock in the morning.'

'That tallies with the approximate time of her death given in the autopsy report.'

'But at one in the morning Dyana had already been gone for a long time. And there's no question of her having come back without my hearing her. I always hear footsteps on the stairs, and she was wearing boots!'

'What time was it when you saw her leave?'

'Immediately after her quarrel with Denis: I told you.'

'Shortly before eleven o'clock?'

'Yes.'

'Interesting! Quite a coincidence. Exactly the same time as Mademoiselle Claire was, or rather, was not telephoning Colmar.'

Loiseau made no comment. His eyes were fixed on Claire and light slowly dawned on him. 'Good God, you mean . . . '

'Yes, Loiseau. It wasn't Dyana you saw. It was Claire in a red wig, wearing Dyana's clothes.'

'Then where was Dyana?'

'At home. Put into a deep sleep by a strong sedative.'

'Who gave her the sedative?'

'Claire herself, when she came up at nine! The quarrel she had with her father was solely to give her an excuse to leave the meeting, go upstairs, have a drink with Dyana, and slip the dope into her glass when she wasn't looking.'

'Are you saying that my daughter deliberately provoked the quarrel?' Wotan asked.

'Yes, that's what I'm saying.'

'And, in a way, manipulated me?'

'No, no, I'm not insinuating anything of the sort. There
was a piece of play-acting, but two people took part in it.'

'What's that supposed to mean?'

'It means, my dear Grün, that the master-mind behind
the whole scheme *was you! It couldn't have been anyone but you!*
It was you who conceived it, devised it and worked out
every detail. With something approaching genius! And, of
course, with your daughter as your accomplice and your
son as . . . executioner.'

'It can't be true!' Edwige stammered out desperately.
'It just can't, Monsieur Dullac!'

'I'm afraid it is, madame,' Dullac told her gently.
'You've only to listen while I give the full account of what
happened. I mentioned, a short while ago, the discrepancy I detected in Jacques Schiller's statement and Martine Blitz's. But it wasn't the only one. Not by any means.
And it was those discrepancies that finally put me on the
right track. For instance, Denis Grün was described to me
as being very puritanical, with a strict code of morals, yet I
was asked to believe that he refused to marry Dyana. And
a second discrepancy: Edwige, Jacques and Martine, all
three of them well-acquainted with Dyana, said it was she
and not Denis who was reluctant to marry. Now, who
maintained the opposite? The three Grüns, father, son
and daughter. Others did so, too – Alice de Potztausend,
for instance, but she scarcely knew Dyana and was only

repeating the three Grüns' official version. Third and last
discrepancy: I was told that the father and children didn't
get on, that they never stopped squabbling; but Edwige,
who ought to know what she's talking about, claimed that
it was just a game, something they indulged in for their
own amusement, and that the three Grüns were really as
thick as thieves. And I've proof that Edwige was telling
the truth; for when there was a difference of opinion between the members of the discussion group, whose side
did Claire take? The rebels, whose views she shared? Not a
bit of it! Her father's!

'What it's important to understand is that, despite
some superficial differences of opinion, those three beings
were one and the same being, and that this three-headed hydra
bore a single name: Grün! For them, it had the same
connotation: their family and their house. And that's why
Dyana is dead: because she had put the House of Grün in
danger.

'Wetzel unknowingly gave me the solution to the mystery when he told me that, a year ago, Wotan had gone
through a bad period financially. He had wanted to buy
his failing business from him; then, suddenly and miracu-
lously, Wotan brought off a highly profitable sale that put
him on his feet again.'

'Do you mean that the sale never took place?' Loiseau
asked.

'Precisely.'

'Then how did Grün find the money?'

'Dyana lent it to him.'

'Dyana! Dyana was the poorest of the lot of them,' Martine objected.

'Not last year,' Dullac said. 'Didn't you tell me that you crossed the frontier once to play German lotto? That piece of information stuck in my memory: I made some inquiries, and verified what I'd suspected.'

'Do you mean she won? She'd have told me if she had!'

'Unfortunately, she didn't tell you. And that was a fatal mistake. After hearing the good news, she went straight home, that's to say, to the Grüns'. There she ran into Claire, and, bubbling over with delight, told her what had happened. And to these two young girls – for Dyana was very good-hearted – there was only one thing to do with the money: get Wotan out of his financial difficulties. Wotan accepted Dyana's offer, but begged her not to tell anyone. He thought he would appear ridiculous if Strasbourg learnt that he owed his solvency to the "foreigner", who had come from no one knew where, and whom he had often sneered at. Dyana generously agreed to keep quiet: even Edwige wouldn't be told. Only the three Grüns would know. But though Dyana was generous she was no fool. She was lending the money, not giving it. And she wanted some security for it. What security? Wotan asked. The flat on the second floor was the answer. During the two years she'd been living there and paying rent she'd become attached to it. Wotan had no choice: he agreed. After all, as Dyana was going to marry Denis, it would remain in the family. And at worst he would be in a position to pay back the loan in a year's time, which Dyana had set as the limit. So the young girl found herself in possession of a document signed by the three Grüns: the father and his two heirs.

'Unfortunately, during the following months, the

relationship between Dyana and her fiancé deteriorated. She talked of leaving him, and demanded the return of her loan. Wotan's business had only partly recovered, and he wasn't in a position to repay Dyana, who then decided to sell. To sell! That would mean dividing up the House of Grün, in other words, the beginning of the end! And, at the same time, Denis resentfully saw himself losing Dyana. The idea of murdering her thrust itself forward as the only solution. Everything had to be meticulously planned, down to the last detail.

'To start with, they spread the myth that it was Dyana who was longing to get married and Denis who was holding back: then followed it up with further red herrings. The dispute among the members of the discussion group provided one: they invented another. Claire dropped a hint to Martine, and to Dyana herself, about the fabrication of gold. They'd even go to the length of staging a false burglary, which, incidentally, would yield a profit, since they'd claim from the insurance company for the articles supposedly stolen, while selling them on the quiet later on.

'When they came to the murder itself, they enlisted the services of an ideal witness: a retired police officer above all suspicion who, by a lucky chance, had rented the second-floor studio flat. The three accomplices had noticed, as I did, myself, that Monsieur Loiseau is in the habit of opening his door whenever anyone leaves Dyana's flat or enters it. That was to prove useful to them, too.

'Events were precipitated. On returning from Paris, Claire heard Dyana say to Martine: "One of these days

I'll tell you something." That had to mean that she was getting ready to sell and leave Strasbourg. There was no time to lose: the murder was set for Thursday evening.

'Shortly after the proceedings had started at the discussion group's meeting, Claire and her father became involved in a phoney quarrel. Claire stormed out of the room, went up to Dyana and dropped a soporific into her glass. I know there's a soporific of some kind in the house because I heard Wotan order some to be given to Denis. An hour later, Claire went downstairs again after making certain that Loiseau saw her saying goodbye to Dyana on the landing. Dyana went back into her flat, and a short time later, under the influence of the drug, was fast asleep. Just before half-past ten Denis came back to the house, said goodbye to Charles Feldmann, and went up to the second floor. Once there, it was vital for him to ensure that Loiseau was not asleep, and had heard him come up. So he rang the police officer's door-bell on the pretext of borrowing some aspirin. Then he went into his own flat; some minutes later Loiseau was to hear quite distinctly the sounds of a quarrel between Denis and his mistress.'

'But how was that possible if Dyana was asleep?' Loiseau asked, frowning. 'I could swear I heard her voice.'

'Didn't you tell me that the young couple often quarrelled?'

'Yes, that's so.'

'And on the day that we went into Denis's flat together, didn't we have a chance to admire his stereo *and his tape-recorder?*'

'I get you!' Holz broke in.

Loiseau was still frowning.

'What you heard, Monsieur Loiseau, was the recording of a previous quarrel.'

'To think he'd play a trick like that on me!' Loiseau said, disgusted.

'By this time the discussion group had broken up. Claire helped Edwige a little with the tidying up, then took off her dress in her bedroom on the first floor and, in her underclothes and barefooted, so as to make no noise on the stone steps, went up to her brother's flat on the second floor, where he was waiting for her. With the speed of a quick-change artiste she slipped into Dyana's clothes, put on a wig, snatched up the handbag, and, as the recording came to an end, left the flat again, slamming the door behind her, and rushed down the staircase without putting on the light. As the accomplices had reckoned, you opened your door and caught a glimpse of what you took to be a familiar figure. After that you would be prepared to swear that Dyana Pasquier left her flat, alive and well, just before eleven o'clock. What actually occurred is that the false Dyana went into the first-floor flat, changed back into Claire's clothes and appearance, and ran to the Weberstub, which she reached in a matter of minutes, but a trifle out of breath. It was this that gave the head waiter the impression that she was "a little worked-up": the fact was that she had been running!

'That was the end of Claire's part in the proceedings and the beginning of Denis's. He joined you in your flat to pour out his troubles and provide himself with an alibi. At one o'clock, on the pretext of showing you a letter, he went back to his own flat for a few brief moments; but they were sufficient to enable him to drown Dyana in the bath he had filled beforehand. Then he returned to you and remained with you until the time of death, as the autopsy would determine it, was long past.

'End of act two. Beginning of act three. The Grüns returned from the Weberstub. Edwige went to sleep immediately and heard nothing for the simple reason that her husband had doctored her drink in the restaurant. You may recall that she said she was very tired and in a hurry to get to bed. Shortly after three o'clock, Wotan went up to Denis's flat in his socks. The two men dressed the body in the clothes that Claire had borrowed. Then comes the shock! Denis confessed to his father that he had lost his head and applied too much pressure. Wotan cursed his son's incompetence. He had counted on Dyana's death being attributable to suicide during a fit of depression. What would be the outcome if the autopsy disclosed the marks on the deceased's neck? I guessed that when I thought back to the bitterness with which Wotan told me last Saturday morning, "If you ever do catch the murderer, it'll be entirely due to that blunder." He was thinking of his son. The son who had let him down.

'What could be done? Nothing; it was too late. They'd have to go through with the original plan. Wotan slipped out into the dark with Dyana's body over his shoulder and threw it into the river. Denis and Claire tried to get some sleep: he stayed up and watched. Through the shutters, he saw Madame Dickbauch discover the body and gather a crowd around her. Then – an extraordinary stroke of luck! – he observed everyone move off to Gräber's bar. And a brilliant idea occurred to him. With Dyana's body discovered where it was, so close to the house, if the marks on the neck came to light, proving that she had been murdered, suspicion was bound to fall on the Grün family. So this man of iron decided to attempt a remarkable double-bluff. He went out again, dragged Dyana out of the river and deposited her in his own workroom! When the body was discovered for the second time, and some twenty witnesses swore to having previously seen it in the river, it would be obvious that some ill-disposed person wanted to incriminate the Grüns. To confuse the trail still further, Wotan set the scene for the fake burglary as originally intended. Then he went upstairs to bed again, and when I rang the front-door bell at six o'clock he had no difficulty in acting a man who's half-asleep: he had not slept a wink all night, and it had been the most taxing one of his life!'

Dullac broke off there. In a deathly silence, everyone present turned to look, frozen with horror, at the gigantic, black-clad figure of the pitiless murderer.

As he made no comment, Dullac inquired, 'Was my reconstruction accurate, Grün?'

'Remarkably so, my friend: particularly as you had so little to go on,' Wotan answered urbanely. 'It was Denis's anxiety to get back to Loiseau as quickly as possible that caused him to lose his self-control and press down too heavily on Dyana's neck, leaving marks scarcely visible to the naked eye, but which, if discovered, *would furnish irrefutable proof that she had been murdered.* Poor Denis!'

'Yes, poor Denis!' Dullac agreed. 'For then his insufferable torment began. Torn between his growing terror of being found out, and the genuine grief he felt at Dyana's death, he went completely to pieces. I was right in thinking that his nervous prostration was not a pretence, but I failed to realize what underlay it. Meanwhile, Wotan, you had another of your brilliant ideas. To mislead me further you planned to make it appear that it was *you* that someone had a grievance against and that Dyana had only been killed *in order to make you suffer*. So, on Monday night, you persuaded your wife to go to the Weberstub with you. From your kitchen windows there is a clear view on to the Pont Saint-Martin. Claire is a first-class shot and you had in your loft a high-precision rifle that you didn't know I'd seen. Just as you passed under the light from a street-lamp, Claire fired, wounding you only slightly in the shoulder. You were running an enormous risk, but a risk in keeping with your readiness to gamble and the mania that possesses you both. For Denis, it was the last straw. During the night, he hanged himself.'

Loiseau interrupted him. 'Are you telling us that Denis really did commit suicide, after all?'

'Surely it's obvious! It was the only way out left to him. And there, Wotan, your conduct was despicable. You found the letter Denis wrote three years ago, saying goodbye to Dyana, in her handbag. And, once again, you tried to bring off a double-bluff; you placed the extract from the letter, which seemed to point to suicide, near Denis's body, counting on us to submit it to our experts and learn that it had been written three years earlier, which would then convince us that it was a case of murder! Because, if we had concluded that it was suicide, you ran the risk of our surmising what the real cause of it had been.'

'Do you actually believe that the death of my son, my

only son, meant nothing to me?' Wotan demanded indignantly.

'It didn't stop you turning it to your own advantage,' Dullac retorted.

'That's not true,' a voice broke in. 'It was my idea. My father had no part in it.'

Claire stood up, confronting the detective. A Claire now aggressive and cruel. There was no trace of regret either in her eyes or her voice. How naïve he had been!

'Was it you, too, who planted Jacques's letters in the loft?' he asked.

'Yes, it was. Up till two days ago I was unaware of Jacques's and Edwige's treachery. Then I had a sudden hunch and searched my stepmother's bedroom. I found the letters and thought up a way to use them against her and Jacques.'

'So that they should be arrested instead of you?' Dullac suggested with infinite bitterness.

Savagely, Claire snapped at him, 'It was only what they deserved.'

'Deserved! How do you make that out?'

'*They had dishonoured the Grüns!*'

2

'You made me undergo a very bitter experience, Monsieur Dullac,' Edwige said.

'I know,' Dullac answered. 'But please believe that it wasn't solely from a desire to avenge myself. They made a laughing-stock of me, my self-respect and my feelings.

They took me for a sucker. But they did worse than that earlier on.'

'Why, what did they do?'

'They kept you confined in a cage. Weren't you aware of it?'

'Yes,' she said, 'I was aware of it.'

'Now I've made the three-headed hydra bite the dust and opened the door of your cage. Fly away, madame.'

'I will. Thank you, Monsieur Dullac.'

3

'What's satisfactory about our job,' Holz observed, 'is that it's all mapped out. Rules exist and we carry them out. There's no room for doubts or moral scruples. Personally, I like it.'

Dullac did not answer. He was thinking of Claire.